BOUND BY DESTINY

Cheat Sheet

Character	Wolf	Witch	Nickname
Kayden Miller	Phoenix	N/A	*Kayd*
Kamari Lee-Miller	Tatiana	Penelope	*Kam*
Kayari Miller	Duchess	Tempest	*Kay (Riri by Brady)*
Kamden Miller	Brice	N/A	*Den*
Trinity McCallister	Iliana	N/A	*Trini*
Brady Preston	Raven	N/A	N/A
Roman Rivers	Aeracles	N/A	N/A

Paul (Pack Delta)

Jesse (Pack Omega)

Details:

City of Lovingshire (low-veng-shire)

Cheshire Pack House located on the outskirts of Lovingshire (30-minute drive)

Destiny Falls: located on pack property but a public area

*Warning: Contains strong language and violence.
Trigger warning: mention of rape (discussion only).* *

This is a work of fiction.
Names, characters, places, and incidents either are the product
of the author's imagination or are used fictitiously. Any
resemblance to actual persons, living or dead, events, or
locales are entirely coincidental.

Table of Contents

Thank you to those who took a magical journey through Bound to You and are here to continue the fantasy. I appreciate every one of you.

Thank you to my beta readers:

Thank you for helping me slow down just a bit and make this story so much better.

And now...the journey continues...

So, It Begins

*"**H**i there, my name is Kayari Denise Miller.*

*Yes, my parents ARE Kamari and Kayden Miller. I'm
sure you are aware of their infamous love story...oh god,
please don't make me explain... you are, aren't you?*

sigh Fiiiiine.

*So, my dad met my mom in her art studio, he knew he
loved her the second he laid eyes on her, but he had to
relay one small minor detail...uhh, that he was a
werewolf, and he was the Alpha leader but surprisingly,
she was okay with that. I guess when it comes to love
being a ferocious creature is the least of your worries.*

*They fell in love, had some drama— by the way never
and I mean NEVER mention the name Bridget or John
Michael— any who they got over the drama of the
fighting because my mom totally whooped some...(huh?!,
sorry mom!) She can hear me, but you know what I
mean, she totally kicked butt.*

After that, they got married and had me and my brother Kamden.

Ta da!

That wasn't too painful.

Well, their love story is one for the ages while mine...it's an interesting matter. Let's begin, shall we?"

"Dad, it's crazy and unheard of! A pack has never had two Alphas, an Alpha and Beta yes, but never two Alphas! This isn't going to work; we try to kill each other every chance we get but you want us to share leading the pack?!"

Kamden shakes his head frustratingly and Kayari's mouth is wide open, but no words come out. Their dad just gave them the worst news of their teenaged life. They were going to share the responsibilities for their pack, the almighty Cheshire pack.

Share?! They barely shared the womb peacefully let alone their toys growing up.

There have been a lot of changes to old traditions since their mother, Kamari discovered she wasn't human but a Violet Legacy. Legacies are one of the most dominant creatures in the world. She was born half-white witch/half-werewolf and combined with her husband's wolf they created the most powerful children in the world.

Kayari gained her mom's powerful wolf/witch combo and Kamden inherited his dad's supreme wolf abilities.

Kam and Kayd decided against a lot of ancient traditions, including leaving the children with a human family member. They wanted their lives to be as normal as it could be which is why he had a school built on pack grounds. They would learn the human world, but their main focus was strengthening their future warriors.

But this news he just relayed was anything but normal.

"Listen you two, we've gone against a lot of protocols, and I think you and your sister can share the title instead of one being Alpha and the other Beta. We can't choose between you, you both equally possess the power and characteristics of an Alpha so you will share the title, that's final!"

"But...!" They both shout as their parents walk away.

Kam stops Kayd in the hallway, wrapping her arms around his waist. "Honey, do you think we made the right decision? Maybe one of them would have been okay as Beta."

He kisses her forehead. "They were meant to be equally great and this is how we guarantee the longevity of our pack. There will be some growing pains, but I know this will work."

She leans up for a kiss. "You better hope so or I'll never let you hear the end of it."

He wraps his arms around her. "Soon, it'll just be you, me, and a beach for a few weeks...I can't wait to see you in a bikini, especially the red one with the..."

She covers his mouth by bringing him down for another kiss, this one slow and sensual. "Even after all these years you and Phoenix are still horn dogs."

P: Damn right and she's lucky you're in control because we wouldn't be talking right now.

Kayd shakes his head trying to clean it up. "Phoenix says not with the hot, sexy mate we were blessed with. I love you, baby doll."

She grins wide, her cheeks flushed. "I love you, too and I know what he said was *far* more sexual than you're letting on, Kaydy."

He groans, after all this time her pet name still causes him to cringe, but he loved her.

Two Alphas?!

"How can you be so damn calm?! This is madness Kay! How are we going to share a responsibility as big as this?! I think dad has finally lost it."

Kamden groans all his frustration out, then grabs his favorite comfort food, Cool Ranch Doritos.

"You better lay off Den, or you're going to weigh 500 pounds and the ladies won't be swooning over you anymore. You'll lose your playboy status!"

Kay laughs as he snarls and walks out of the kitchen with the bag.

Kay shrugs her shoulders to the big reveal, she didn't know what to make of this decision from her parents. Her mind was elsewhere, she was far more focused on secretly finding her mate. She didn't want any interference from her twin or her parents.

The story of her parent's love put a twinkle in Kayari's eye, she was just like her mother, she wanted that everlasting love, but she also wanted the challenge of being Alpha to their pack. She knew her dad loved them equally and tried not to make a contest of things, but she never saw this coming.

The twins were approaching their 18th birthday, when he would pass the reins over to them, apparently together.

How would this even work?

This was something that she would have to seriously sit down and discuss with her brother but not right now.

Right now, she was daydreaming in her room about her mate, what he would look like if he would be from another pack because she's met most of the guys in her pack and the pickings were slim to nonexistent. Being a powerful creature also didn't make the guys approach her, most were afraid of her father and like most dads he relished in it, keeping his baby girl to himself.

Most of the she-wolves there were vicious when it came to finding their mate or just their next target. Kay didn't have the energy to entertain that mess.

Besides, she had a better chance of finding her mate at the transfer of power ceremony when packs from all over would come to witness this one-of-a-kind ceremony and celebrate.

It was a huge deal when pack leaders handed their reins over to their heir and now that their dad broke the news of them sharing, this ceremony was certain to be witnessed by all, it was unheard of and there would be scrutiny and curiosity as to how this would work.

How would the great Miller children share the rein and more importantly, will they succeed?

She was certain once word got out there would be talk, lies, and rumors. The naysayers will swear they will fail and then a competing pack would be so bold as to try to attack thinking they are vulnerable, but that won't happen, it can't.

Kamden and Kayari Miller were no ordinary heirs. Not only does Alpha blood course through them but also Legacy magic. The Moon Goddess herself made their mother special and passed it on to them.

"Kay!" Her mother's voice shakes her out of her thoughts.

"In my room, mom!" Her mother opens her door and finds her lying on her bed gazing at the ceiling.

"You could have just linked me, mom. No need to yell." She rolls over to make room for her. Kam kisses her forehead admiring the facial features of her daughter. She was stunning with her dad's emerald green eyes but with her mother's distinct hazel ring surrounding them. She also inherited his bone structure with her mother's flawless brown skin and curly locks. She knew the minute she saw her that she would be a heartbreaker.

"You know I'm old school, we yell for our kids, none of this mind link stuff before I knew what I was. Anyways, what's going on with you? Are you okay with your father's decision for you to share the Alpha title with Kamden? You know we only want..."

"You only want the best for us, we know, mom. You've always told us that. You don't want one to feel superior to the other. Honestly, my brother and I have a lot to talk about when it comes to that just not right now, I think he's still shocked and to be quite honest, pissed."

Kam exhales, "Well, hopefully, your father is talking to him right now. We all know Kamden can hold a grudge like no other." Kayari shakes her head in agreement, she knew all too well.

One year, Kay had filled his precious black-on-black Mustang with rainbow confetti as a prank, she thought it was harmless until she saw his reaction, he was livid. It took him weeks to get rid of all the confetti. He screamed about the damage to the face value then ignored her for two weeks. No one could get him to crack until she wrote him an apology letter and paid for four full details so the professionals could restore it back to mint condition. She's seen and felt his bad side and frankly, she wasn't willing to see it again.

"Mom? Do you think I'll find my mate soon?"

Kam caresses her daughter's face. She also inherited her mom's ache for true love. Her sweet girl has seen her parents' love and swooned every time they would tell the tale of how they fell in love. She certainly was her mother's child, she yearned for someone to walk up to her, wrap their arms around her and simply state, "You're mine," resulting in her head swimming and heart bursting knowing she had found her one.

Kayari shakes her head and focuses back on her conversation.

"Oh sweetheart, of course you will, you are caring, beautiful and powerful, your mate will be damned lucky to find you."

She sighs and drops her shoulders. "I hope so..."

Kam pulls her daughter's chin up to eye level; she sensed a bit of hopelessness in her reply. "Hey, what's going on, baby girl?"

Kay notices the concern in her mother's eyes. "It's nothing, just thinking about my future after dad dropped this bombshell on us."

Kam takes her hand. "Yeah, I know it's crazy but your father's and my whole life together has been just that, a wild ride. What I wouldn't have given for a normal day but then I think how what we experienced shaped us for the better. Finding out about being a Legacy, honing my powers then finding out I was pregnant with you two, THAT incident, and so much more have crossed our paths during your father's reign but one thing we are certain of is that you will be great leaders. I have complete faith in you and your brother, so much so the day after the ceremony your father and I will be on our way to Santorini for some us time. Perhaps now is a perfect time to work on a sibling."

Kayari almost tumbles off her bed. "Eww, mom! My child-like essence...please, don't you think Den and I were enough? I beg of you, no more Miller offspring."

She kisses her forehead, "Okay, I'm just joking, no more siblings. Besides, I could never have more wonderful kids as I do right now. I love you both so much, you're the light of our lives. Now, come help me with dinner, tonight is lamb chops." Kay groans as she drags herself off her bed to help her mom.

Understanding

"**H**e's insane Brady, like my dad should be committed! How do you share the Alpha title, it's pure insanity!"

He stares at his best friend, dialed in on Skype, looking for some sort of agreement. After a few prolonged seconds of silence, Den clears his throat.

"Hello?! Looking for some advice here!"

Brady rubs his hands over his face. "I mean what can I say Den? He is still Alpha, and he said the decision is final, so work with Kay and run this pack, that's it. We're depending on you and as legend says you guys are the strongest beings on this Earth so you should be able to rule just fine. Give it a chance, she's just as capable as you. You guys have been making history since before you were born."

With a call from his stepmother, Brady hops off Skype. Den just sighs as he contemplates how this is going to work. How can this pack be run by two Alpha heirs?

Dinner was quiet tonight with the announcement still looming in the air. Kayd observed both children and realized only Den seemed to still be quite upset, using more force than needed to pierce the delectable portions of meat that his mom cooked to perfection. It was a testimony to Den's unhappiness, and he made sure everyone was aware. Kam could hear Kayd sighing at the whole situation.

K: Honey, you knew they weren't going to just take the news with a smile on their face, we expected this, please understand what he's feeling.

Kayden: Baby, how can I when he won't talk to me? He's two feet from me and my son won't even look me in the eye. It's frustrating, can't he see how special they are?! I see so much potential. I know my kids; they're destined to be great leaders. It may be unorthodox but it's going to work! I just wish they would see what I see in them...

He groans out his frustration.

D: I do dad, I know you have this vision for Kay and me, it just made me feel like you don't trust one of us ruling alone. I know you want us to know that we are equal. It's going to take some time, but we will make you proud, I promise.

Kayd physically reacts to his son's linked words sending a small smile his way and he returns it.

Kayd: You already make me proud son, every single day. If I didn't trust you, I wouldn't be so eager to pass the baton. Besides, I need some quality time with your mom, it's been so long since we...

Kay: OMG, dad! Shut up, shut up, shut up! We don't want to hear about whatever you and mom have planned. Gross...

They all laugh out loud to the silent conversation. Kay is still shaking her head, disturbed that she chose that moment to link into the family talk.

"Well, pre-Alpha training starts tomorrow for you two to start understanding and strengthening your powers, especially you Kay, before you receive your witch powers you need to establish rules immediately, we learned that lesson the hard way.

P: And what's THAT supposed to mean? You tell lover boy I saved his ass out there! The nerve...

Kam takes his hand as her eyes flash violet. "Let's not piss off Penelope, please. You know she can hear you." He quickly kisses her forehead, looking past Kam.

"I'm sorry Penelope, without your help I wouldn't be here, I know that. I merely want Kay to establish her relationship with Tempest before any need arises. Forgive me..."

Penelope rolls her eyes and dismisses the whole situation with a wave of her hand.

P: Whatever. You're lucky you're freaking cute.

Kam laughs out loud as he looks at her in question. "She says you're lucky you're cute."

He squeezes her hand and smiles. "I'm lucky to just have you, baby doll."

Kayd and Kam don't even realize they're alone until after their make-out session.

"Oh, when did they leave?" Kayd flashes that playboy smile as he grabs her by the waist pulling her to his lap.

"Who cares, now I finally have you all to myself."

Training

Kay lingered around the corner watching her lovebird parents. She loved seeing them fawn over each other, it was adorable.

She wasn't the least bit worried about taking over the pack with her brother, she was looking forward to it.

She admired her brother, she may have been the oldest by a few minutes, but it was Kamden whose strength shone through every action he took. His stature was like an Alpha, he strategized like an Alpha, and he exuded all those leadership qualities of past Alphas, she wanted to be like him which is why she was okay with sharing, she would learn it all from her brother, the model Alpha.

A yawn catches her off guard as she notices the time, 10 pm, no doubt they would have to report to the pack training center at 5 am. Dad was a stickler for an early morning exercise session, he always said it was a great start to the day.

Den is lying on his bed reflecting over today's events. Even though he expressed hesitation he knew if he had to co-reign that his sister was perfect. She was beautiful, noble, regal, she held an air about her that screamed grace and nobility. She could negotiate with the cruelest Alpha to give her whatever she wanted. She had her mother's beauty and all the qualities of a superb Luna. They would use those qualities she possessed when his hot temper and threats didn't work. She was the yin to his yang.

Bzzzzz bzzzzz

Kay huffs loudly as she forces one eye open to read the time. The LED flashed 430 am.

"Ugh, sometimes I really hate dad for his early morning sessions."

She peels herself out of bed and slugs towards the shower. Turning it on to a temperature that reflects the current hell she's in, she peels off her clothes and hops in with a shriek.

"Ooh! Hot hot hot! Ahhh...perfect."

She stands under the showerhead and relaxes in the warm massage she's receiving, lightening her grumpy mood only slightly.

After 10 minutes, she hops out and quickly dresses to resist the change in temperature. She puts on her favorite black capris and purple sports bra with a white sweatshirt crop top. She tosses on her matching purple trainers, grabs a towel, and she heads out her bedroom door.

She walks into the kitchen to grab a granola bar to find Den nodding off on the counter. Grabbing the granola bar, she couldn't resist slamming her hands on the countertop.

"Den! Get up, we have to report to the training center."

He jolts up, almost knocking himself off the barstool. He glares at her.

"Jeez Kay, you almost gave me a heart attack. Not cool, sis."

She pats his back and smiles her most innocent smile, the one she uses on Dad when she wants something her way.

"But you love me, you have to, I'm your co-Alpha."

He takes his orange juice and places the cold bottle on her neck, shocking her.

"AHHH! What the hell, Den?! Seriously? You're a jerk!"

He grins as he gets away from her clutches. "But you love me, I'm your co-Alpha!" He laughs too hard for her liking as she chases him out the door towards the training house.

You could hear a pin drop as Kayden paced the stage looking out at all the young wolves up early for training.

After "the incident" with his wife, Kayd made training a top priority for the pack. Even though she took care of the issue herself he did not want to risk her, or the kids being hurt, so he arranges group training at least once a month for all able-bodied pack members.

All eyes watched him as he paced the length of the stage in his usual white t-shirt and black shorts, some of the new girls Kay's age giggled. She knew her dad was handsome and that girls would have a crush on him, but it was still awkward and definitely annoying.

"Mmm...If I were only a few years older, our Alpha is so hot. I bet he's an animal in bed." A girl whispered to her group of friends, Kay couldn't help but to turn around and lock eyes, warning her.

"I suggest you keep that trap shut and focus on the training. I know your dial is set to whore, sweetie, but if you could keep it down most of us are trying to learn from my father, who is VERY happily married by the way."

The girl's face dropped and was about four shades redder, she was new to the pack and didn't know anything about her family or their story. She lowers her head as Kay turns back around to listen to her dad.

"The most important thing to learn is that you represent the strongest pack on the planet, the Cheshire pack has gone through hell and back to become what it is! Most of you know the story of how my Luna and I met and her Legacy status, making our children infinitely stronger. Kayari and Kamden, please join me up here..."

Kay looks at Den as they both slowly make their way up to the stage.

Kay: What is he doing? It's too early to be put on display.

Den shrugs his shoulders as they lock eyes. She groans as she makes her way through the crowd. Her father offers his hand so that she can hop on stage.

"Now, many of you know that my time as Alpha will be ending and the dilemma is who will be my replacement. You know that our twins have been given equal opportunity for everything, we do not put one above the other and when I decided on the Alpha position, I kept that logic. I want my warriors to be the first to meet your co-Alphas."

There were loud audible gasps followed by whispers. The most audible questions heard were, "How does that work?" "Can he do that?" The murmuring grew louder as he tried to explain. He whistles to gather their attention.

"Listen, I know this is something unheard of and it will be an adjustment, but I have the utmost faith in my children to uphold the same morals that have kept this pack strong and relatively untouched. We will have several town hall meetings before the formal ceremony to address any concerns and answer any questions. But until then I am still in charge and I want everyone to partner up and run through the drill."

He nudges Kay to Den suggesting they stay on stage and do their combat practice. They assume protective and combative positions as all eyes are on them.

Kay whisper yells to her brother. "Did you know he would announce it here?!"

"What? No! But it's not necessarily a terrible thing, look whatever happens we are in this together, I know we fight all the time but honestly Kay, you're the only person I trust with pack business, I wouldn't want anyone else." His revelation makes her smile, catching her off guard as he sweeps her feet and she lands on the ground with a thud.

"Den, you asshole!" She screams causing everyone to stop.

He laughs out loud, "Thank the Moon Goddess you'll be an Alpha because that is NOT the mouth of a proper Luna!"

He pulls her up and she punches his shoulder hard leaving a bruise. Then a thought surfaces, will they have a single Beta, or do they each need one? There are so many questions, she cannot focus on the training.

"Den, we really need to flush this out, I can't concentrate when I have so many questions on how we will make this work. Let's talk after lunch, please." He could see the genuine concern on her face.

"Okay, sis, after lunch, but for now..." He swipes her leg again putting her on the ground, but she grabs his leg with her arm and brings him down hard. He groans and she rolls on top to pin his shoulders.

"Getting sloppy are we, brother?" She kisses his forehead to further irritate him. "Tsk, tsk... "

K

Kayd watches his children during their combat training. He shakes his head at their bickering, but he smiles.

"This is going to work, I know it, they are smart like their mother and strong like me. Moon Goddess, I can feel it in my heart. I just need your blessing."

He closes his eyes in prayer as a pair of hands wrap around him as a hug from behind. Judging by the sparks he knew it was his very reason for living.

"Hey handsome, when do I get my one-on-one training, I was promised by this overly sexy man this...*personal*...training."

When he turns around, she is biting her lip in a way that makes his heart race and his blood rush south. He whines as he looks down. "Baby doll..." She pecks his lips and smiles slyly.

"Our room, ten minutes...or I am starting without you." She walks away without giving him a chance to respond.

His eyes glued to the sway of her hips rocking side to side as she heads back to the main house, her scent spellbinding, and although no one can hear she is relentlessly teasing him through their Legacy link and not the pack link.

He clears his throat. "Alright, take two laps to the falls and back and you will be done with training for today." Kay thought she heard her father growl as he made his way behind her mother.

Kay shakes her head, "That's what I want...my parent's love." She smiles as her best friend Trini taps her shoulder as she catches up to her pace in the pack.

"This news is crazy, Kay! How long have you known? Do you think you and your brother can do this? Wait...Why are you smiling so wide?"

She shakes off the thought of her parents. "Trini you're my best friend, right? You know me better than anyone outside of my family and while I am thankful to be sharing the crown with my brother, I can't help but wonder what is going to happen if I find my mate. That's the most important thing to me, I want that love my parent's share. It's been two years since I gained my senses to find my mate and... nothing. Maybe I'm not meant to be with anyone." She shrugs her shoulders and her demeanor is slightly somber.

"Not a chance Kay. You are an Alpha female, you're like prime real estate, you can't just be with some Joe Schmoe, he must be special to understand you and all you have. You are the child of a Violet Legacy, you are part white witch and werewolf, and now you share the title of Alpha with your brother, girl that's a lot to take in! Your mate is probably a prominent King or another powerful Alpha or what if it is another Legacy child?! That would be crazy!"

Kay scoffs "It wouldn't matter what he does as long as I was the love of his life."

As they are talking Kay runs violently into the group who has stopped just shy of the Falls and the border.

"Oof! What the hell man, why did every--"

Sssshhhh! Someone whispers.

Den takes a protective stance around Kay as he sniffs the air. "Tell dad there are rogues nearby. I can smell those slimy bastards!" Den then walks forward through the crowd as Kay links her dad.

Kay: Dad! There are rogues near the Falls, call Uncle Brent, Evan, and Miles!

Kayden: We're aware and on our way sweetie, just get back to the house with your mom and the other women and children.

She huffs.

Really? Unbelievable.

Kay: Why?! Because I'm a girl, because you don't think I can handle myself? Thanks for the vote of confidence, father.

She cuts off the link and orders the group to take a combative stance as they watch the shadows move between the trees in the forest. Den is ahead of the group eyeing the movement as he uses his Alpha voice to growl, giving them a warning. They take it to heart as they disperse towards the mountains. Perhaps they were just scavengers, or they were scouting the grounds, testing the pack reflexes.

Kayd and her uncles join the group not a moment later. "Why the hell are you all still here? Everyone back to the house, NOW!" His Alpha voice booming through them causes fear in their eyes as they scramble towards the house.

Miles, Brent, and Evan shift and fan out to secure the perimeter with the security detail.

Den brings up the rear of the crowd and Kayd tugs his daughter's arm to face him. She stares him down with the fire of the Moon Goddess behind her eyes. She shifts her weight.

"What, Dad?!"

He is caught off guard by her attitude.

"Kayari Denise, what is wrong with you?"

"Don't call me that, just moments ago you said that my brother and I are strong enough to lead this pack but the MOMENT it is in trouble you want me to cower with the women and children. What the hell, dad?! I have been training for years to defend myself, you say we are changing the rules of how we lead this pack until you feel your daughter might be in danger and want to shelter her, it's not the 1920's dad, I can take care of myself!"

She finishes with tears in her eyes, all she could do was shake her head in disappointment. She walks away without another word.

I Just Want to Protect You

Kayd groans because he can feel the

disappointment behind him. He knew her arms were crossed, and her anger was high, in fact, he could feel it radiating from her person. He was going to hear it whether he wanted to or not. He turns to face the judge, jury, and executioner that is his wife.

"Kayden James Miller, what did you say to our daughter?!"

He sighs loudly. "Ughhhh…listen, baby doll, I... I just didn't want her to get hurt, she's my baby girl, my only girl!"

She only shakes her head. "You said she was strong enough to rule with her brother, don't treat her as a delicate little flower, that girl is the result of two highly stubborn people. You gave her the title and soon the pack, do not go back on your word. You know she can do this; she can take care of herself." She folds her arms across her chest at their original position awaiting his reply.

He drags his hands over his face and lets out a combination growl/groan/sigh. "You're right, I know she can fend for herself, but she will always be my princess. I can't help but want to protect her..."

"I know, but what happens when she finds her mate? It'll then be his job to care for her and will you be able to let her go then? Don't smother her, let her grow. Let's head back, security can take care of this and the report."

He takes her hand and with big doleful eyes says, "There's no way to finish what we started earlier is there?" He squeezes her hand gently but judging by her stoic expression, he was out of luck.

"Not a snowball's chance in hell after what you did to our daughter. And you better fix it, Kaydy, or face long term consequences. Remember the ninth-grade dance argument? You bet your ass you do."

What she is referring to is during the kid's ninth-grade year, a boy named Nathaniel asked little fresh-faced Kayari to his school's dance. She came home excited, but her father quickly forbade it because he was from one of the rival packs and he didn't believe his intentions. Kayd always had his guard up when it came to infiltration of the pack even by a snot-nosed almost teenage boy with raging hormones. The way a dad's mind works is amazing when it comes to his only daughter.

Anyway, after he explicitly forbade her, Kam and Kayd had an awful fallout and she threatened to leave him to his own devices. Needless to say, he let her go and it went well without incident. He spent days after that getting back in his wife's good graces and it was not so easy.

Back in her room, Kay is face down, crying in her pillow as Trini rubs her back. She holds her head up, "I don't get it, one minute he thinks I'm competent and the next he's treating me as if I am going to break at any moment. This world is still sexist as hell no matter what we do. I should just give the title to Kamden since that's what dad wants anyway, male rule. He just thinks I'm a liability." She resumes crying into her pillow.

"Kayari! That is just not true, sweetie." She looks back to see her father, slightly heartbroken.

Trini walks out of her room, to the kitchen where most of the teenagers hung out.

She turns back around and huffs in her pillow. "Admit it, dad, times have not changed. You don't want me in power, it's 'too dangerous' and I'm too delicate, just give the crown to Den and leave me alone. I don't care anymore."

Her body jerks indicating she was crying, openly sobbing into her pillow. He pulls her into him and makes sure she looks into his eyes. Looking at her tear-stained face pained him, he never wanted to be the reason for her tears.

"Princess, I know if given the opportunity, you could rule this pack alone without anyone's assistance and would do an excellent job. You are the combination of your strong-willed mother and bull-headed father. I know I say things that sound incredibly sexist, but I don't mean it in that way. I am just a father who is terribly protective of his only daughter. I don't want to lose you to anything if I can prevent it, but I have to realize that soon I won't be the man in your life. Some handsome devil will take you from me and you'll go off and have a family of your own."

She can see tears well in his eyes and it softens her heart. She immediately wraps her arms around her dad, hugging him tightly.

"No, daddy! I'll always be your baby girl, your princess! No man is going to change that, you'll still have my love but..." She looks away, catching his attention.

"But what? You can tell me anything, sweetheart." He takes her hand and she smiles slightly.

"You know when you and mom act all lovey-dovey all the time? I want that, daddy, I want someone to love me the way you love mom. But it's been two years...and... I just...I want my happiness too but maybe...it'll never come?"

Now tears reemerge as he kisses her forehead. He remembers those feelings of hopelessness and heartache and though he wanted to shield her from it he knew he had to be honest but considerate.

"You know it took me quite a while to find your mother and I get it; believe me I do. But you need to be patient, I don't want you to end up in a situation that resulted in my confrontation with your late Uncle. Patience is key, my heart, your mate is out there and when he discovers you, he'll know what an amazing catch you are! And then daddy gets to threaten his life if he ever hurts his baby girl."

"Daaaaad..." They share a laugh as he hugs her a bit tighter.

"It's what daddy's do, protect their princesses. Now, I need you to work out your command structure with Den."

She jumps up in a huff, "I forgot! I was supposed to talk to him after lunch! I got to run dad; I love you!" He can hear her feet running down the hall towards her brother's room.

A voice clears their throat behind him to catch his attention. "Now...I think you have earned a make-up session from earlier.

Ven a la cama te necesito tanto (come to bed, I need you so bad)."

He turns to see his wife at the door. She knew what to say to rile him, it was how she said it and the inflection in her voice, it was dripping with lust.

"Vamos muñeca, deja de molestar... (come on baby doll, stop teasing)" He winked at her, after nearly twenty years he was almost fluent. She purrs at him.

His growl was low as he eyes her like a prize. "Don't start what you can't finish, I'm already quite wound up from earlier."

She smiles and pushes herself off the door jamb, "Well, come on mi amor, time's a wasting. Your Spanish is getting so much better, sounds so...enticing." She squeals when she finds he is chasing her down to their room.

Congrats

"**O**h sweet Moon Goddess, why do you give me exceptional hearing just to hear my parents flirting with each other?! This is truly a gift and a curse."

Den shakes his head furiously, turning up his radio as Kay just chuckles. They both heard their parent's spirited conversation, but she was too focused on the big task at hand, besides she was smart enough to block the link early in their flirting.

"Focus, Den! First, let me say even though it was a shock, there is no one I would want beside me other than you. You're already what an Alpha should be, and I want you to teach me to be as strong as you, especially when things get tough."

He smiles, genuinely taken back by her honesty.

"Well, if we're being honest then you also have to teach me your grace, patience, and civility. You can negotiate your way out of anything, remember the glue gun incident? Somehow, we manage to escape with our butts intact with only a week being grounded, and even then, they let us off after five days. Had it been me I'd not exist right now but somehow you got mom and dad calm enough to see your point. I could have never done that."

"So, we have a lot to learn including whatever dad is going to teach us, but we need to decide a few things now, including the Beta situation. Should we each get a Beta, or do we only have one that'll act as tiebreaker in our arguments, someone who is fair? I mean Brady is fair and I would consent to him as our Beta. Trini can be an advisor because let's face it, she is no fighter."

Den was speechless. "Really, you'd be okay with that? See, you already know how to make everything make sense. Okay, and we can bestow the advisor role to Trini. We can work on our Delta and Omega later."

They spend a few more hours discussing, writing down their ideas and chain of command, and changes to already set processes.

Later in the kitchen, they reveal their decision to Trini and Brady.

Trini squeals in excitement. "I'm so excited to be your advisor, I did NOT want to be Beta, that's too much work. Congrats to you, Brady, you are perfect for the role. I guess you'll be spending more time around Kay, huh?"

He coughs at the statement that catches both him and Kay off guard.

Brady smiles at Kay, she can feel the blush rise on her cheeks.

Brady Preston was something worth looking at. He stood six-foot-four with auburn hair and porcelain blue eyes, he was the typical teenage male who spent his days in the gym sculpting the perfect physique and boy, did he have it. If he ever decided to grace that beautiful body with tattoos it would have the ideal canvas.

Kay snaps out of it when Brady goes to hug her, catching her entirely off guard. She takes the opportunity to inhale his scent and it was magical, he smelled like the beach on a rainy day. She noticed he held the hug a few seconds longer than usual and his breathing was erratic... *weird, right?*

She lets go and his eyes meet hers, she notices his chest was rising and falling quicker than normal, like after running wind sprints. He was trying to calm his breathing back down.

He clears his throat and smirks when he finally releases her. "Congrats again on becoming Alpha, Riri."

Brady was the only person to call her Riri, it was his pet name for her. She never questioned it, she just thought he was teasing her but now there was an air of something in the way he said it, was it interest, lust? No, it couldn't be, he wasn't her mate so why would he be interested in her, he could have any girl.

"T-thank you, Brady." She choked out, noticing the obvious awkwardness in the moment.

Immediately, Trini pulls Kay up to her room, saying they should lounge poolside and need to go find bathing suits.

In her walk-in closet, Kay decides which bathing suit to wear while she throws her white one-piece with daring side cutouts to Trini.

"Umm, so what was THAT a moment ago?"

She blushes again, trying to play it off. "What do you mean?"

Trini chucks her shirt at Kay's head, hitting her hard.

"Oh, come on! Don't act innocent there was a lot of tension between you and Brady, sexual tension, man it was so thick you could cut it with a knife. He IS one fine specimen too and he has always seemed to have liked you like that for a while now."

She scoffs. "He does not, besides he's my brother's best friend and you don't cross that line. I will admit that he is absolutely handsome Trin, but he isn't my mate. He's just trying to make some other girl jealous or catch their attention with me as bait. He probably thinks of me as his annoying little sister, that's why he's always picking and ragging on me."

Trini looks shocked at her excuse and rolls her eyes. "First, no one would do that because you are super gorgeous and all the girls are already jealous of you and two, there was no one there besides the four of us, so who was he trying to make jealous, huh? Yeah, I thought so. And, might I add, the way he looks at you is not as a little sister. Even if he isn't your mate, you can still have some fun in the meantime, no need to go all nun on me. Have some fun, live a little because once you become Alpha it's all business from there."

She shakes her head, "That's not true, me and Den make the rules so if we want to have fun we can!" Trini rolls her eyes at her optimism while Kay chooses a yellow two-piece, grabs her towel and sunglasses, tosses on her jean shorts unbuttoned and they head to the pool.

C oming down the stairs and through the kitchen to

reach the pool, the guys catch sight of the girls. Kay notices that Brady's eyes do not wander away from her body and he bites his lip. She reaches for the mini cooler from the top shelf of the pantry to fill it with ice as Trini grabs the drinks and some snacks. The ice maker produces more ice than room in the cooler and a few pieces tumble to the floor. She sets the cooler on the counter as she bends over to grab the rogue cubes. As she was in that position, she heard a low growling but didn't find the source, so she shrugs it off as she makes her way back to standing. She places them in the sink and grabs the cooler.

"Are you guys going to join us? You know you want to..." Trini asks as she displays her million-dollar smile, it has a hint of mischief. Truth is that Trini always had a crush on Kay's brother and wanted to make him want her and that's why she wore the sheerest cover-up that covered absolutely nothing. Her body filled out that swimsuit better than Kay could as if it were created for her. Trini was built like a model but with a little added cushion in all the right places, she may have been considered short but that didn't cut down on her big personality. She swung her hips and pouted her luscious lips in Den's direction as she walked out. Den was aware and drank a large amount of water to douse the fire.

Kamden was currently uninterested in finding his mate, he just wanted to enjoy life and have fun. He was in no way going to avoid it but, in the meantime, he would not feel bad for hanging out and sleeping with other girls. Typical playboy behavior.

Kay, on the other hand, was still untouched in about everything, except the kiss from Roman Rivers at their junior high school prom. He was six foot one, long dark hair he wore in a man bun, the quintessential bad boy persona. During the perfect slow song, he placed his finger underneath her chin and lifted it so that when he leaned down just a bit their lips met. It was some kiss. "Wow" was all she could utter, and he just smiled his bad boy smile.

She never saw him after that, rumor has it his family had moved to California that same night.

She shakes herself out of her daydream to see Den shrug his shoulders nonchalantly and follow them out. Kay finds her way to a sun chair and removes her shorts and sits to apply sunscreen, her slight sweat kissed skin was in desperate need of some vitamin D. She feels like she is being watched and sure enough, she looks over to see Brady eyeing her.

"What?"

He smiles. "Nothing, you look pretty."

He immediately looked away so she couldn't see him blush. She sits back against the chair, her arm over her head and she sighs adjusting her legs, one leg bent at the knee, to get more comfortable. His words reverberate in her mind, but she ignores them and focuses on getting some rays.

She slides on her shades as she notices Brady taking off his shirt. She couldn't help but stare at his back muscles flexing as he shrugged off his white t-shirt. He turned and sat back in the chair next to her, rubbing his chest and abs with sunscreen.

She quickly averts her eyes to the diving board where her brother stood about to perform some over the top stunt that would make the she-wolves swoon. He does a double somersault backflip off the board with minimal splash and gets applause and whistles from the girls who were already sunbathing, some topless.

Shameless, she thought.

Kay opens the cooler and looks back at Brady. "You want a soda?" He nods and she hands it to him. She yells at Trini who is eyeing her brother like the last piece of dessert at the table. She looks flustered as the girls surround the ladder he must inevitably use to get out of the pool.

She huffs as she slides on her oversized glasses and saunters over to a new addition to the pack. His name was Orion and he was a classically handsome guy. He was super tall, standing at six-foot-nine dwarfing Trini's five-foot-six frame, he had deep brown eyes and sandy brown hair. He had several large tattoos that covered his body to include the one on his chest that traveled over his shoulder and across his back. He told her it took 22 hours to complete it.

Trini was obviously using Orion to make Den jealous as she leaned into him and touched his tattoos. He wrapped his arms around her waist and picked her up, she squealed in surprise.

"Oh Orion, put me down you handsome stud!" He flexes his muscles and she is all over him.

"Only if you agree to dinner tonight gorgeous,

I'll take you somewhere real nice." She agrees and he sets her down, putting his number into her cell phone and she texts him so he can have hers.

She turns around and walks away from Orion who was clearly watching the sway in her hips as she turned around to him and winked, but so was Den. His hands fisted tightly at his sides; he ignored all the girls surrounding him to watch Trini with the new guy. He was not happy when she pulled out her phone from her bikini top to hand it to him. She giggled and flirted with him heavily, placing her hand on her chest and flashing her beautiful smile at him.

Den always thought Trini was gorgeous, stunning really, but he was too afraid to pursue her because she was his sister's best friend and that is muddy territory. If you screw up, you will have hell to pay from your sister and still have to see her hanging around the house.

Trini continues to exaggerate the sway of her hips past Den and sits next to Kay. Kay chuckles and hands her a soda. "You are the absolute worst Trin, he about had a heart attack when you were talking to that guy and then when he picked you up into his strong arms...done!"

She pops the top and smiles. "Who? Orion? He's a sweetheart, that's all. I can't make your brother see the catch I am so until then I plan to have fun, too. Well, my date is in three hours. I should go get ready; I'll text you...after." She winks and waves before walking off.

By then Den has some cheap blonde who is all but grinding in his lap. She was trying hard to grab his attention, but his focus was on Trin walking away.

Kay: When are you going to admit that you like her?

Den: The same moment you realize you like Brady.

Kay: I do not, he's not even my mate so...

Den: Cut the crap Kay, we are in an era of new rules we may not even have mates so what are you going to be lonely the rest of your life and wait for that fairy tale?

Kay: I prefer to wait, Den. You can go around and sleep with anyone if you want but you're only hurting yourself. Do what you want, playboy, just know that my best friend is head over heels over you and I won't allow you

to keep hurting her. I'm glad she's going out with Orion;
he'll show her the attention you won't. Enjoy bleach
blonde bimbo over there...I'm sure Trini will thoroughly
be enjoying Orion...

With that she shuts off the link and huffs, storming away
from her frustrating brother and his loose morals. She
didn't even realize she also left Brady; he could only
watch her disappear into the house.

Brady continued to flip a coin between his fingers as he
always did when he was nervous or in deep thought. He
didn't want to hurt anybody...especially her...

Not My Mate

She slams her door, rattling the walls.

"UGH!!! What is so wrong with wanting to wait for the one meant for you alone? What is the point of sleeping around besides increasing your chances of catching something? I shouldn't feel bad holding on to my standards, they're mine. Why are people questioning my decisions already?!" She flops into her bed and screams into the pillow.

"Sweetheart, you know we can hear you, right?" She looks back to see her parents. They sit on the side of her bed.

"Is this about your brother?"

She signs "Yeah but not about pack business, this is about love. I'm sick of him flirting with all those skanky girls when he knows that Trini likes him, I have no idea what she sees in him but that's not the point. She likes him and not because he's about to be Alpha, she's genuine. Then he says that I like Brady, but I don't, he's not my mate and I don't do casual relationships like him. I just don't understand."

Kayden slowly backs away and leaves this issue to his wife. Kam links him that he's in so much trouble before she focuses back on her daughter.

"Sweetheart you and your brother may be twins, but you are two different people who look at things differently, including love. He may just be afraid or maybe he just isn't interested in finding his mate just yet and that's okay. You have to let your brother make his own path and if it leads to Trini then so be it, but you can't force him to be something he's not."

She huffs, "So he can be a manwhore and you're okay with it?!"

"Kayari! Don't use that language towards your brother!"

"But he is, mom, if I were like that, they'd be calling me all kinds of names. Classic double standard!"

She throws her hands up in frustration.

Her mother sighs. "Whatever the case may be you have to let your brother live his life and whatever happens, happens. Just like he can't force you to open your eyes, neither can you."

With that she leaves Kayari to her thoughts.

"Whatever, Brady's not my mate...he's not my mate..." She closed her eyes; she needed a quick nap to forget this terrible day.

The ocean air was crisp with a hint of salt, Kay was wearing a skimpy red bikini and a white knit cover up. She felt so exposed and so covered at the same time, but the covering was the sparks and tingles she felt every time they touched. She was lying on her back before she was awakened by a voice. "So, how does my baby love the ocean?" She sees her hand in someone else's. A pair of lips meet her hand. "I love you, sweetheart, finding you was the best thing to ever happen to me..."

Kay is startled awake as the voice trails off. She catches herself before she face plants onto the floor. She was panting hard "Wow, that felt so real. I wonder who he was?" She gets herself together before lying back on her bed thinking about the mystery man. The one thing that stood out was how familiar his voice sounded...

"Five miles and practice will be over, get to it! No shifting!"

Den rolls his eyes at his dad's barking as he bursts into a sprint with Kay right behind him.

"I don't see why we need extra training...we haven't had an incident in months!"

Kay edges in front of Den and he increases his speed to lessen the gap.

"Yeah, but we don't know what these packs have up their sleeves, we are a constant target especially when this news breaks globally. I don't plan on losing our rank or our pack and I know you feel the same." She nods as she gets winded on the three-and-a-half-mile mark.

When they return Kayd clicks the stopwatch. "Not bad, you shaved off 38 seconds. You are getting faster and stronger with each session, I am so proud of you guys now go hit the showers, you reek."

They glance at each other before tackling their dad for a hug. He fights for a second then gives in to the love of his kids.

"Dammit, just tell me! I don't understand! Why are you doing this to me? To her?! Can't you see this is already killing me, to not be able to touch her and feel what I am supposed to feel, to pretend like everything's okay?! It's not...it's not okay!"

There was a long silent pause. "Tell her and she is dead then what will you have without your precious mate...stick to your orders and it'll all be over soon..." And with that the line went dead.

Brady drops the coin he had been flipping and buries his face in his hands. He didn't have a choice, he needed to keep her safe.

"**G**irl! We haven't gone shopping for your party dress and the party is in... three days! It's going to be the event of the year...well until your culmination then THAT will be the event of the century. Let's go to the mall to find you something...I don't know, spectacular!"

Kay protests. "I'm not really in the mood to shop."

Trini shakes her head furiously. "Nope, no way, uh uh, now you are going shopping for your party. No arguments, you've been holed up in this house for too long, let's...go!" Giving Kay no room to argue she gets up and grabs her purse on the way out.

As they head towards the front door, Den and Brady come out from the kitchen. Den is shamelessly shirtless with his sunglasses perched on top of his head and Brady was wearing his button up open. They had obviously been lounging poolside.

Den pops the top on a soda, "Where you guys off to?"

Trini stops and turns around flashing her gorgeous smile. "If you must know, we are going to the mall to find

Kay's dress for the party, she's going to look so hot every male coming won't be able to resist her. Her mate is going to melt from her hotness."

There was a faint growl, Kay looked for the source but couldn't find it.

"Anyway, we've got to go find the sexiest dresses in town, later boys!" Trini grabs Kay and they head out the door.

Den turns to Brady, "Dude, did you just growl?"

"No man, it wasn't me. Maybe it was someone in the kitchen."

Brady plops down on the couch in the media room rubbing his temples. "You okay, B?"

He looks at his best friend and forces a smile. "Yeah, I'm fine just...tired is all. Did you guys already send out the invites and notify the packs?"

He nods while plopping down, "Yeah looks like the Mystic, Pinnacle, and Falcon pack are sending people, still haven't heard from Ice Passage or Cold Mine pack but either way, we are already looking at 300+ people which means great chances of meeting some new...options." Den wiggles his eyebrows and nudges his friends' shoulder.

Brady scoffs, "Is that all you think about? The next conquest? You're worried about your next lay when you know that Trini is into you and really likes you, for you, not because you're about to be the next Alpha, which is all those girls care about out there at the pool. Wake up man and give the girl a chance. Some people never meet their mate or circumstances beyond their control keep them from them. Just...think about it. I got some errands to run. I'll catch you later." And with that Brady leaves a confused and stunned Den behind.

But Brady didn't have any errands to run and he found himself parked at the mall. He was walking along, store by store hoping to run into them "by accident". He ordered a strawberry shake from Burger King and continued walking around until he spotted Trini sitting near the dressing room of a fancy boutique with her mouth wide open. When he turned in the direction of her shock he could see why.

There, standing on a pedestal surrounded by mirrors, in a short gold backless dress was Kayari, she turns to face away from the mirror, looking at the detail of the low back, fringe bordered the back and hem giving the dress movement, but it also emphasized her beautiful skin, her ample bottom, and her statuesque legs. He was seconds away from dropping the shake but caught himself. He boldly walked into the shop as they were talking.

"Are you kidding me, Kay?! You look amazing, like ridiculously hot! Besides, it's your 18th birthday you're supposed to be celebrating becoming a legal adult."

"Trini, it's too much, I feel so exposed. It's not my type of dress besides, who am I supposed to be impressing?"

"Every single red-blooded wolf in a hundred-mile radius! You are prime real estate my friend and there are going to be some fine options there. In fact, a little birdie told me that Roman will be there...yes, your old crush who gave you your first kiss, that Roman, I bet he's gotten even sexier since then and he was hot way back then." Trini starts fanning herself.

"But he lives all the way in Cali, why would he come here just for my birthday? Though...it would be nice to see what he looks like after all this time. He was adorable back then." Kay looks at the dress once more in the mirror.

"Hmm, this dress is insanely sexy and fits me right but it's not the right one for the party, but I will buy it for a future event. Oh boy if my dad saw me in this..."

As she takes a final look in the mirror, shaking from side to side watching the fringe, her eyes fall on Brady standing behind Trini but slightly out of the way where Trini doesn't notice. She smirks and he smiles.

"Well, I think you look absolutely stunning." His deep-voiced reply makes Trini jump.

"Holy hell Brady! What's with the sneaking up and why are you here?"

She throws him a questionable look as he casually sips his milkshake.

He shrugs, "I needed to get away from my pea-brained best friend talking about his potential conquests from this party. Tired of hearing it..."

Trini's eyebrows raised. "Really? I thought birds of a feather flock together and you'd be happy of all the new females roaming around."

He turns away and before he is out of sight he glances back. "Not all of us are here for the conquest, some of us are still looking for the real thing, the long term. Perhaps...already finding it..."

His gaze focuses on Kay one last time before waving over his shoulder, "Adios, ladies, see you at the party."

Trini turns back to Kay, but she holds up her hand. "Before you even utter a single syllable, he is NOT my mate, no tingles, no sparks, nothing. It's just harmless flirting but I'm not looking for that and you know it."

Trini shakes her head, her brow furrowed in deep thought, "No Kay, there's something there, he's trying to avoid it or something I can tell but he can't resist being around you either. I'd keep an open mind about our Brady Preston."

Kay just shakes her head as she makes her way back into her dressing room unaware that Brady was still close enough to hear their conversation.

He pulls a bottle from his jacket pocket, takes out a pill and sighs, putting the bottle back, and taking the pill. He takes one last glance at her before heading out of the mall. He needed a quiet place to think...to come up with a plan.

The girls come back with bags and bags of items when they run into her dad. "Why do I feel my wallet has been ransacked just by looking at all of that?" He couldn't say no to his baby girl.

"Daddy, I only spent two grand and most of that was for things I needed, the party dress was only $400." She hands him back his credit card with a kiss on the cheek. "Thank you, daddy, you're the best!"

"I know." Just as he was about to put the card away Kam snatches it from his grasp.

"I also need a new dress for this party...unless you want me to wear the little black number from New Year's Eve..." That elicited a vicious growl from him, he remembered that dress, how could he forget how it hugged her curves and gained the attention of every male there.

"Not a chance, I don't want everyone eye humping my wife again. That dress should have been illegal, it was so damn sexy on you. I should have torn it to shreds when I ripped it off you."

He pauses for a moment and they both look down.

She gasps. "Oh my, did I do that? Sorry, dear, I must go. You know what to think about...I'll make it up to you when I get back, I promise." She places a gentle kiss on his lips.

He looks heartbroken as he tries to use the old saying "Think of dead kittens, dead kittens." She's already out the door and he repeats it like a mantra walking to their bedroom.

"Why are you keeping me from her?! What does this have to do with her being Alpha, you still have to get rid of her brother too to weaken the pack. Just tell me why?! I've done everything you've asked of me up until now, I've taken these stupid pills...please..." Brady is almost in tears as he pleads with the mysterious voice on the phone.

"Legacies gain their powers once they meet their mates and are marked so keeping her from you keeps her weak and vulnerable enough to overthrow the pack, so you will continue to take your pill to mask yourself until we can overthrow those Miller bastards and become the all supreme pack. If you alert her in any way, we will kill her with no remorse, all evidence will point to you and her family will rip you apart. Just act normal...you'll hear from us soon." And the phone line goes dead. He shakes his head in frustration.

"But I love her..."

(Somewhere far away)

"Is he still protesting? If we don't attack soon, we'll lose our chance, we need to put everything in motion if we are to cause the fall of the almighty Cheshire pack." He taps his fingers against the chair as he looks out the window.

She grins and places her hands on his shoulders, massaging his angst and stress away, kissing his cheek.

"Don't worry, he won't go against his orders, he can't...who says no to their mother?"

It's Melody!

T he house was bustling as many teams of people

were setting up for Kay and Den's 18th birthday and
culmination ceremony. Kayd had decided to do both at
the same time, he was more than excited to be going on
vacation with his wife, their bags already packed.

Kay was lounging on her balcony, her blue-green kaftan
blowing in the wind since she was going to be
practically bound in her dress, she kept it casual but
sexy. She kept thinking of incidents these past few
weeks involving Brady. She finally realizes what Trini
was talking about, he would get close to her and then
pull away. He was constantly staring at her during
combat practice or any other time they were in the same
room, but he never made a move. It was all just so
confusing, she could feel what she described as this
weak pull, but it wasn't the sparks and explosions you're
supposed to feel when you meet your mate, but she was
also a Legacy heir so maybe it was different with her?
Either way, she was torn between her own emotions,
does she wait for those sparks or explore with someone
she found attractive in the meantime?

She also had been having the mate dream over and over
only adding a bit more information each time. This last

episode the mystery man had kissed her hand and squeezed it gently. He sighed and whispered,

"You have no idea how long I've been waiting to be with you, I love you so much Kayari Denise Miller."

His final words gave her goosebumps when she woke up. His voice, she couldn't quite put her finger on it, but it was eerily familiar but comforting. She shook the thought away and stood against the railing looking down on the massive front yard when something caught her eye.

The same girl who was eye humping her dad during combat training was now playfully touchy with Brady. She twirled her hair and giggled at everything he said, finding little ways to touch him.

"So, are you going with anyone to this party? Maybe...I'll see you there and we can have some fun later...alone?" She pushes her boobs forward to catch his attention more and Kay scoffs, turning around, she has seen enough. But before she could completely disappear out of sight unnoticed, Brady catches a glimpse of her walking off. He pulls back from the girl who seems hurt at his retraction.

"Where are you going? I thought...maybe you can meet me at the falls, and we can go skinny dipping?" Her touch feels wrong and he recoils, trying to get away from her.

"S-sorry Laura, Lauren, Lily, whatever your name is, I'm not interested, excuse me." He pulls his shades up and walks into the house.

"It's Melody!" She screams out but he doesn't care as he scurries inside.

Just as he closes the door Kay comes down and their eyes meet. He keeps his jaw from dropping as her legs peek out from the slits of the kaftan, she was outrageously sexy, and she knew it. Her platform sandals clicked down the stairs.

"Riri...how are you?"

He nervously asks, trying to gauge her emotional state as she continues down the stairs.

"I am *just* fine, Mr. Preston, don't let me keep you from your fan, I merely came down to grab some water before I start getting ready for *my* party..."

He could feel the sting in her words, and he wanted to blurt out everything right there, but he couldn't risk her life.

"She doesn't mean anything to me, Ri, I couldn't even get her damn name right."

She shrugs, no change to her expression, "It is of no concern to me, I mean we are not together Brady so you can be just like my brother and whore around, looks like you're more alike than I thought."

Ouch.

Her words were malicious, he thought he was nothing like his best friend, especially not when it comes to women. He could feel the anger rising to the surface.

"You know what, Kayari, contrary to your belief, I am not looking to sleep with every girl in town. Men look for their mates too, don't judge me if you don't really know me or my situation. Enjoy your party."

She instantly regretted her words, "Wait, Brady, I'm sorry. I don't know why seeing you with her bothered me like that, but I shouldn't have been so nasty. Please say you're still coming tonight?" She looks up at him with her beautiful hazel bordered green eyes filled with hope.

"Enjoy your party, Kay...and congrats again." He turns around and walks out the door.

She watches him turn and leave, the door closing slowly. He didn't use his pet name for her, no, he just called her Kay and her heart sank.

"Brady..." She says to herself.

As she drags herself back up to her room, she feels nothing but guilt. She flops onto her bed face first and groans. "What is wrong with me?!"

"Hmm, you want the long version or the short?" She turns to see Trini holding two cups from her favorite smoothie place. "Here, because there will be no real food for a long time. What's with the heartbroken face? Kay...what did you do?"

She takes the smoothie and sits up on her bed. "Okay, I-I-I don't know Trini, one minute I was okay just getting some fresh air on the balcony but then I saw that tramp who was talking about my dad flirting with Brady and...I felt hurt, kind of and I walked away but he obviously saw me and ran up to me as I was going to the kitchen and I was so mean, Trini, I don't even know why but I said some things I shouldn't have and I don't think he is coming tonight because of my stupid filter-less mouth."

Trini sits at her vanity and crosses her legs. "Are you finally ready to admit your feelings or do I have to watch you sulk all night?"

Kay buries her face and groans into the pillow. "I don't even know what this is!!! It feels like I like him, but it feels stifled like it's blocked by a barrier but some of it managed to still get through. OMG...I don't even know what I am saying...I'll feel awful if he decides not to show up especially because Den would expect him there as his best friend and his-I mean, *our* Beta."

"Well, as your Advisor, I recommend you start getting ready, we can sort all that out later. Come on birthday girl, time to celebrate!" She wiggles and dances wildly to no music, making Kay laugh uncontrollably. She uses the remote to turn on some music before heading into the bathroom.

A hand lands hard across Brady's face, enough to knock him to his knee. His eyes stay peeled to the ground below.

"I told you to keep taking your pills! This cannot work unless you do what I tell you to! Don't you love me, Brady? Don't you want to make your dear mother happy?"

He looks up with tears in his eyes, looking at the very woman who gave birth to him.

"But why, mama? Why are you against me being with my mate, she's all I can think about, I can mask my scent but not my feelings for her. I need her, I love her...your sick delusion has nothing to do with me, leave me out of this, or kill me but I love her. Kayari IS the love of my life."

His mother squeezes his face roughly, her nails drawing blood.

"That little spoiled bitch is unworthy of love, her family ruined my life, OUR lives and I plan on making them pay!"

Brady

He roars, standing up to face off against his

mother, baring his teeth.

"You will watch your words, mother. Hmph!
MOTHER... I shouldn't even call you something you
never were. So, Carolyn, THIS is over, WE are over.
You're not my mother, in fact, Gracie has been more of a
mother to me than you ever were and now I know why.
Your obsession has gone crazy...she's gone! If you ask
me, Aunt Bridget deserved to die! She was going to kill
a woman and her innocent children for a weak, pathetic,
pitiful excuse of a man who rejected her, twice! How
miserable and desperate do you---"

His mother once again slaps him hard enough for him to
briefly lose his temper and his eyes turn black as his
wolf, Raven, starts to surface. His hurt, disappointment,
and hatred turned into a vicious roar, full of rage and
anger.

Without another word he shifts into his wolf, running out
and heading home to his father and stepmother. His
anger had hit its boiling point when she talked about his
mate and her family, how dare she when she abandoned
him and his father to pursue revenge.

Raven was panting as he hit top speed, his auburn fur rustling in the wind. When he reached the house, he pulled on a pair of shorts and a black t-shirt he stashed by the door.

He opens the door to see them cuddled up watching their favorite cooking show.

The day that Carolyn walked away from them was the most heartbreaking moment that he and his father shared. The pain he watched his father bear was agonizing. Blessed with a second chance, his father met Gracie at the local bookshop as they were looking for the same copy of Catcher in the Rye. They took it slow as he told her about the circumstances before she came into his life and then one day, they shared the sparks and he knew that the Moon Goddess had granted him a second mate, a fair chance at real love. He prayed for her, for a woman whose heart was as big as her beautiful smile.

"Hey son, what are you up to?" He pats the seat next to him and he sits down when his father wraps his arm around his shoulder.

"Nothing much, dad, just had to let Raven out for a run."

His father checks his watch, "Isn't it about time to start getting ready for the party and your culmination as Beta of the pack?"

Brady lets out an audible distressed sigh. "Yeah, about that, I don't think I am going."

His stepmother takes his hand. "Why, what happened, and what happened to your face?" She lightly brushes the marks near his cheeks, but they were healing.

He forgot about the torture his "mother" inflicted upon his face.

"Well, I was running through the forest, must've hit some branches on my way back, it doesn't hurt though. Anyway, Riri and I had an argument and we both said some hurtful things and I just don't think I should ruin her night being there if she doesn't want me there."

His dad is watching his son's movement. "This night may be mainly about them, but it is also about you assuming your role, too. You and Kamden have been the best support team to each other especially since your mother's disappearance. That little spat with Kay was just a lover's quarrel."

Brady shoots up. "What?!"

His parents laugh. "Oh, Brady you can't be naive, that girl has liked you for years, the blind can see that. Let me take a wild guess at what happened, you were talking to or flirting with another girl and she saw you." He was amazed at how spot on she was.

"I--"

She puts her hand up. "Brady, I can't tell you what to do or how to act but I can tell you both care for each other, how you deal with it is up to you, but you can't hide forever." She kisses his forehead and gives him a small smile. "I'm going to start getting ready."

He drops his head in his hands and groans. "UGHHHHH..."

His dad chuckles as he takes a sip of his beer. "She was spot on, huh? I knew it because you both show the same behavior when you are around each other. I don't know why you won't pursue her, but you need to figure it out before someone else comes and sweeps her off her feet and you'll be left with a lot of what-ifs."

If his dad knew what was going on, including Carolyn trying to use him to exact her revenge but he needed to keep her safe, he'd die if any harm came to her. He needed a new plan since he knew she would try anything now that he was no longer under her control.

His shoulders slump. "I'm not her mate, dad." He winced as he let the words slip out, "so it doesn't matter. She is meant for someone better than me, probably another Alpha so they can create some super pack."

His dad sighs and pats him on the back. "Don't bend so easily son, I didn't think I'd find happiness after your mother or even get a second chance but here I am. Your story is just beginning...I'm going to get ready, too."

Once again Brady is left alone with his thoughts, if anything he had to go to keep eyes on her, he didn't trust his mom or Alpha Damien, her mate. But he wasn't, his dad was her mate and after the death of her sister, she lost all wifely and motherly instincts.

Brady shakes his head, does he go to the party, or does he stay? Yes, Kay was upset but only because he hadn't taken his pill and it was probably wearing off so she could feel a slight pull at her heartstrings. It wasn't her fault and he needed to let her know that. He went to his room to get ready for the party.

Ready for the Ball

Kay yells from her vanity as she finishes up her makeup. "Trinity, are you almost done?!" Her makeup choice was bold and daring, her eyes smoky to emphasize her green orbs and the perfect red lip, she only needed a brush of bronzer to enhance the radiance in her skin.

Her bathroom door swings open and Trini is standing in a long emerald green dress that had a high offset split highlighting her toned legs. Both the neckline and split were embellished with a ruffle accent. She pulled her hair up into a stylish bun with some wispy pieces to frame her face. Her silver heels catch the light to shine and sparkle like a diamond.

"Well, what do you think?" Trini does a slow turn as Kay stands up, her mouth wide open.

"Wow, Trinity you look absolutely stunning. Just gorgeous best friend! Now switch places, I need to get dressed."

Trini hits her on her butt when she steps past. "Let's go best friend, we're about to make these men fall at our feet, especially my sexy birthday girl! OWW!"

Fifteen minutes later Kay opens the door performing the same slow turn.

"Well...hot damn, Kay you are going to kill someone looking that freaking hot!"

She steps out in a long red spaghetti strap, high split dress. Much like Trini's she had a ruffle accent on the train of the dress and one that crossed the bodice highlighting her cleavage perfectly. She walked over and sat on her bed to put on her strappy silver heels. She decides to wear her natural curls down, a silver choker, and diamond earrings. She stands up and looks in the mirror.

"Is it too much? Maybe I should have gotten the white lace dress..." She looks flustered and her friend places her hands on her shoulders.

"Calm down, you are a 20 on a 10 scale, absolutely stunning, even if you don't find your mate, you'll find tons of interest, guaranteed."

Kay sighs, she doesn't want that, she wants someone in particular. She is still reeling from her argument from earlier.

"I just hope Brady comes..." She mumbles not realizing she said it out loud.

"Of course, he will..." Trini gives her a knowing look as she crosses her legs before continuing.

"Oh, that boy definitely likes you, if he sprinted away and didn't even know the girl's name, I'd say he was more interested in what you were doing. I don't get why you two don't just give in."

She shrugs. "Something odd has been happening lately, I can't fake like it isn't, but I don't know what to do after I basically called him a whore to his face." She drops her head and Trini hugs her trying to comfort her.

"Let's enjoy the party, I am certain he'll be here because he cares far too much to not be even after a silly fight. Don't worry, babe, he'll be here." She nodded in agreement, but she wasn't so sure.

They meet Kamden in the hallway before the grand staircase. He wore a burgundy smoker's jacket with black lapels, dress pants, and a black button-up and just like his father, no tie. He looked devilishly handsome with his jet-black hair slicked straight back unlike his usual off to the side. He takes notice of his sister and then Trini. His jaw drops at the sight of them.

"Wow, you both look breathtaking..."

He takes his sister's hand and twirls her to get the full view.

"No one will be able to resist you tonight."

She smiles but thinks about the incident and her smile fades.

He places his hand on her face, "What's wrong?", but she doesn't say anything. She walks back into her room as Trini gives him the details of what happened.

What *was* happening, why did she feel so upset suddenly? She felt a mild panic attack coming on as she placed her hand over her heart, feeling the rapid beating until a hand laid gently on her shoulder. She turns around about to explain to Den what happened, but her mouth suddenly became dry when her gaze was not upon her brother but Brady, a handsomely dressed Brady.

He wore a dark obsidian blue suit with a matching dark blue button-up, his hair styled to the opposite of his usual, giving him a more charming appearance. He placed a hand in his pocket as he gazed at her from top to bottom.

"Wow, Riri you look..." He clutches his chest. "you absolutely take my breath away."

Immediately she hugs him, catching him by surprise, but he embraces her soft, ample body against his.

She looks up at him. "I'm sorry, Brady I shouldn't have said what I said, it was stupid. I shouldn't have judged you. It's just that..."

He places a kiss on her forehead and smiles. "No worries baby girl, just know she didn't mean anything to me." He didn't know why he said it, but it made her feel better.

"Okay." She smiles and he offers his arm.

"Well, let's go celebrate your birthday. I'll be the luckiest man with you on my arm looking like this." She blushes as she wraps her arm around him and they walk out, they meet up with Trini and Den who were talking very intimately. Their exit from Kay's room startled them, causing them to jump back. Kay eyes them suspiciously as Trini was blushing hard.

As they descend the stairs all eyes are on them. She recognizes a few familiar faces, including her favorite aunt, Nessa, and her mate Christian, Brady's parents, and his great uncle and aunt, the same lovely elder couple who loves her mother's artwork, and their Uncles Miles, Evan, and Brent with their wives. She looks to her left to see her parents, her mother teary-eyed, as usual, wiping them away as she gazes at her children.

Waiting to be formally announced by the emcee, they stand at the top of the first level of the staircase.

"Ladies and gentlemen, please welcome our guests of honor and future co-Alphas of the great Cheshire Pack, the Miller Twins, Alpha Kayari, and Alpha Kamden Miller."

Applause rang out as they descended the remaining stairs, greeting their parents. Kayd kisses his daughter on her forehead.

"Dad..."

He looked down into her eyes and smiled innocently. "What? The announcer was your mother's doing!"

Kam pinches his side as he jumps. Her mother looked radiant in a slim and simple black dress with a plunging back, obviously appeasing dad because he didn't want anyone looking at his gorgeous wife.

"My baby girl, you look absolutely beautiful, go...mingle. Don't worry about your old parents."

The Bad Boy

T he first person Kayari runs up to is her Aunt

Nessa.

"Auntie Nessa I've missed you so much!"

She all but tackles her to the ground but Christian holds her up, bracing the impact.

"How is my beautiful niece doing? Sorry Xander couldn't make it but he's in intense Alpha training and his father thought it more important he get ready for that, but he sends his best to you. I must say that dress is lovely, obviously you got your fashion sense from me and not your mother. So, tell me, who was that handsome young man who escorted you down the stairs?" She wiggles her brows.

"Auntie...that's just our Beta, Brady."

Nessa quickly shakes her head. "No darling, the way he was looking at you with you on his arm was not just a Beta duty, that boy loves you. I swear, it's like watching your mother all over again."

Kay immediately blushes looking around to see who may have heard her loud-mouthed aunt. "We're just friends, that's all." Nessa doesn't breach the subject as Christian asks her to dance.

The ballroom was bathed in black and gold, the cake was the centerpiece in its five delectable layers of red velvet and cream cheese frosting, a large "18" placed atop the cake. The dance floor was in the center with tables surrounding it for the older couples to relax and people watch. Den had pulled Trini on the dance floor and her smile was a mile wide.

Kay was observing the party in general when she felt a tap on her shoulder.

"So, what does a guy have to do to get a dance with the beautiful girl who stole his first kiss?" Kay turns around to see a familiar face.

"Roman?" He places his hand on her chin.

"Hello, gorgeous."

She hugs him and he lifts her off the ground, twirling her around.

"Oh my gosh! How are you?!"

He sets her down gently and he straightens out his vest. "Oh, well you know just hanging out with beautiful girls from time to time, but they never seemed to compare to that little pipsqueak girl whose lips stole my first kiss and my heart."

Her eyes widened at his revelation. What she thought was an innocent kiss that everyone has, he read into it differently, much differently.

"What? Roman I, I didn't know..."

He brushes a lock behind her ear causing her to blush. "Well, how could you? I was gone the next night to California, but I always had a crush on you Kay, when you agreed to go to the dance it was the highlight of my life. To dance and talk and just be close to the girl who had my heart was more than enough. I was heartbroken to have left but I'm back now."

Roman was still handsomely charming with numerous tattoos that added to his sexy bad boy persona. He still had a beautiful smile to complement his warm brown eyes, but there was a darkness behind them. They seemed filled with lust as he stood there leering at her.

"Damn, Kay. Fuck, baby, you got so much hotter since the last time I saw you. Wow...you filled out quite nicely." He licks his lips and scratches his stubble lined jaw.

That small gesture caused her to feel a bit uneasy around him, not a red flag but a 'this isn't right' type of feeling so she steps back to gain some space.

"Yeah, thanks Roman, you still look like the handsome bad boy, causing trouble." She grabs her opposite wrist trying to look less awkward, but he notices right away.

His brows knitted, "What is it, Kay? Why are you inching away from me? I thought you liked me...and that maybe we could pick up where we left off...huh?"

She sighs and drops her arms. "It really is great seeing you, Roman, really. I just feel a little uncomfortable with you being so close."

He closes the gap further, "Why? We shared an intimate first among teenagers and it was something that stuck with me forever and I was hoping..."

He was cut off when her attention went down to her waist where a pair of arms hugged her. She felt a small tinge of comfort.

"Hey, baby, they need you on the stage to start the coronation, let's not keep them waiting." He kisses her temple.

Brady eyes Roman and gives him a warning glare, Raven was stirring beneath the surface. She nods to Roman and walks toward the stage and Brady quickly whisper yells to him, "Not now, not ever!", before making his way towards the stage. Raven's anger radiated from his conscious to envelop his entire being. The nerve of whatever his name is, touching what was his, looking at her like she was an object, he was by her side in a flash when he sensed her uneasiness. He came on too forward and fast.

Brady extends his hand to help her to the stage. There stood her parents, both wearing their crowns next to her brother. Beside her dad was a glass case on a pedestal covered by a veil. Her dad waited for everyone to take their seats.

Once there was a considerable hush he began, "Good evening and welcome to the coronation ceremony as I hand over my Alpha title to my son and my daughter. I know this is an unorthodox decision and I want to thank each of my pack members for asking the tough questions during our meetings. You have made me confident that this pack will only grow stronger. Now, will my son and daughter please step forward."

Kayari and Kamden stand side by side looking over the huge crowd in the ballroom. She focuses her attention on her best friend who can't keep still in excitement. She gives her a thumbs up and a wink, causing her to chuckle.

"I, Alpha Kayden James Miller do hereby relinquish my command to my children, now Alpha Kamden Tristan Miller and Alpha Kayari Denise Miller, on this day the Cheshire pack is now in your control. I present to you your crowns."

He lifts the veil to reveal two crowns, they were bronze in color with smoky grey stones embedded in them. They kneel, as her father places them on their head, to be formally crowned. As they rise, the crowd cheers. Their dad hugs and kisses them both on the forehead.

"Make me proud, the pack is your responsibility now."

They step forward and look around as the applause continues until Kamden signals them to quiet down. "Thank you to our father and our mother for showing us how to lead, we will take all we've learned and continue to strengthen our pack. Our first official announcement is introducing our Beta, Brady Preston."

Den holds his hand down to lift his best friend to the stage, Brady brushes against Kayari and she feels that weak pull again causing her to look down where they made contact, and Brady just smirks.

Kay clears her throat, "And I'd like to introduce our Senior Advisor Trinity McCallister." Den offers his hand, causing her to smile as she ascends the stairs. They all stand together as the pack and neighboring packs get first glance at the new reign of power.

Kayd kisses Kam on her temple and exhales. "That's it, we are officially retired, I can't wait, this time tomorrow when we'll be dancing in a nightclub in Santorini acting 21 again..."

She pulls back, "Umm...are you trying to get me drunk there?"

He escorts her off the stage. "Oh no, I want you to remember every steamy detail of those nights. Come on, let's finish packing our flight is in an hour."

Actually, their flight was whenever they were ready, he bought a private jet years ago for emergency Alpha meetings and family trips. They bid their children farewell and head upstairs. Their uncles would be around if they needed guidance.

They Always Find a Way

Trini squeals in Kay's ear, "Your brother finally

asked me out! We're going out tomorrow. Oh my god, I need you to help me pick out what to wear, I'm so excited and so nervous."

Kay takes her hands, "You deserve it, Trin. Ooh, looks like the new Alpha wants to dance with you."

As Trini turns around, she sees Den hold his hand out for her to take. Kay could see the jealous faces of all the girls swooning over her brother but that's too bad because Trini had been waiting for years. He twirls her as the floor opens to make room for them. She loved seeing this softer side of her brother, swooning over her best friend. She hoped it would last but she enjoyed watching them enjoy each other.

Suddenly, a voice clears behind her. "So, do I have to be formal and call you Alpha Kayari from now on, cause it's going to be weird, given our... history." She looks as his hand extends to ask for a dance.

"Brady, you can always call me Riri...you're the only one who does anyway, it's our special bond." She flashes her smile which melts his heart as they move to the dance floor.

"I'm proud of you, Riri, you and Den deserve this. I have no doubt that our pack will remain strong and powerful, especially in your hands."

Something about how he looks at her makes her weak. She feels the pulses shoot through her, but... they couldn't be...could they?

She's suddenly brought out of her thoughts when she feels her throat go dry.

"Thank you, B-brady. Excuse me, I just need to get a drink."

She wiggles out of his grasp and quickly makes her way to the refreshment table where the waiter serves her some punch. By then her pulse was racing and her breathing was labored, she felt a million emotions at once, what was going on?!

Brady looks around trying to find Kay, but a familiar voice draws his attention that makes his heart skip a beat and sends chills down his spine.

"Didn't your mother tell you to keep taking the pills? Seeing that you blatantly disobeyed, we had to take matters into our own hands and come up with a plan B..." He turns around to face Alpha Damien.

"How...how did you get past security; how could they not smell rogue bastard on you?"

He twists Brady's arm and Brady tries not to show weakness or that he was in pain.

"Just like there's a pill to mask your mate scent there's one to mask me being a rogue. I won't warn you again, keep with the plan or she dies. It will be slow and torturous, and I will force you to watch. In the meantime, let this little incident be a lesson to you..."

He lets Brady go and disappears into the crowd.

What did he mean by that?

What incident?

He starts to frantically search for her and remembers her saying she needed a drink...oh no...

"Riri! Kayari!"

He pushes through the crowd towards the refreshment table, he links Kamden asking if he can see her and he says she's standing by the cake table sipping her drink. He tried to link her, but her link was off, he wasn't sure why. The second he sees her she has just set down her drink and she is swaying slightly, her face paling and her breathing becoming rapid, she clutches her chest.

He got in her sight before she whispered, "Brady" and collapsed to the floor.

"Riri! Kayari! Baby, wake up please! Den, Trini! Find the pack doctor. NOW!"

He holds her until the doctor arrives and they quickly take her to the hospital. Her parents were already on the plane headed to Greece, but Den called and informed them of what happened. He told them to go and that he would keep them notified of everything.

B

roken up, Brady replayed her falling into his

arms, unresponsive. He felt guilt and shame, they had gotten to her and right in front of him. He had put her in this danger! How could he be so careless with her?

Den comes out of her room and sighs heavily. Brady and Trini wait on bated breath to hear her diagnosis.

"Doctor said she was drugged with a liquid that keeps her from sensing her mate, probably will last a week or so, but why would they target her, why in that way? When I find out who did this to her, I am going to enjoy ripping them to shreds! NOBODY messes with my sister!" His Alpha voice boomed down the hallway gathering the attention and fear of those present.

His eyes turn black as Brice gains control. Trini puts her hand on his face trying to calm him, "Brice please...give Den back control, I know you're upset but we need to find out everything before we react, please." He closes his eyes and inhales deeply before exhaling all his frustration out. He opens his eyes to a worried looking Trinity. He presses his lips to her hand. "You're right, I'm okay, thank you." He hugs her tight as she rubs soothing circles along his back.

He looks at Brady, "B, why don't you go in, she was asking for you." He perks up as he presses his hand against the door. The machine beeps and hospital sounds made him uneasy, the good thing is it was also a sign that she was okay. Her eyes were closed, sleeping peacefully until the door made a small squeak and her stunning hazel green eyes appeared pulling at his heartstrings.

"Hey, you're here."

He pulls the chair up to her bed and takes her hand, kissing it lightly. "I'm sorry, so...sorry that I wasn't there to stop this. I should have been there! I'm such a terrible ma--" He suddenly stops hoping she doesn't notice. Luckily, she is too busy trying to console him.

"Hey, this isn't your fault and I'm fine. Hopefully, we can find out who attacked me. And why take my ability to find my mate away, that is just cruel. They must know I don't gain my powers until I am marked. Ugh, it's all so frustrating."

He lays his head against their intertwined hands. "I am going to make this right, Riri. If something happened to you..." He couldn't even speak the words, his hands kept shaking, his voice trembling.

She gently strokes his face, soothing him.

"Although it's something particularly important to me, the effects are temporary, I'll be okay, and I'll be able to sense my mate once again. I mean...that's if I have one.

I'm beginning to think I might not, or I would have felt him already, right?" She gives him a small sad smile and shrugs, that sets him off.

He pushes away, the chair scraping against the tile floor and starts pacing, pulling at his hair.

"Dammit, I can't do this anymore! I'm sorry I spent all these years lying to you, all the missed opportunities...all the times you could have been...I'm such a fool, Riri, a stupid fool! All I ever wanted was her to love me like she used to, and she used it to take advantage of me...to hurt you!"

She sits up watching his movements, fearful of his sudden revelation.

"Who?"

It was the only word she could choke out. Something about this announcement caused a pain in her heart. He wanted love from some other female but why? What made her so special? Why did this hurt so much?

He's still pacing frustratingly never meeting her eye when Den and Trini walk in after hearing his raised voice. Kay ignores them and continues her focus on an overly frustrated Brady.

She whimpers, tonight has been so exhausting. "Who is she Brady, and what have you been lying to me about?"

He is overwhelmed by all the lies, secrets, and guilt so he falls to his knees.

"Brady!"

He held a hand up signaling he was fine, he wanted to wallow in self-pity for a moment. He continues to look down in shame, he takes a big breath before exhaling forcefully.

"The vindictive witch I call my mother is very much alive, she's plotting against your family, and she convinced me to take these," He tosses a white bottle on her bed, "they...mask my mate scent. I've been taking them...for a little over two years...I thought I could get her to love me again so we could be a family."

He trails off looking into her eyes as Trini gasps and Den's mouth falls wide open.

"Holy shit! Brady...you ARE her mate, I knew it!" She squeals but everyone else is quiet, scarily quiet.

Kay looks away, grinding her teeth, it was her coping mechanism to this devastating news, the tears flowing down her cheeks. She bites her cheeks before she could gather the strength.

She shakes her head, "Is it true?"

Heartbreak hit him when her eyes met his.

"Two years...you knew how much I've been obsessing on finding my mate, to have my parents' type of love story and you've been right in front of me the whole time...lying to me. GET OUT."

He tries to place his hand on hers, she flinches at his touch and he feels hurt. "Riri, baby please, let me explain."

"GET THE FUCK OUT, NOW! I can't even look at you..." She breaks down in her brother's arms as he tries to calm her down. Her body wracked in sobs after hearing his betrayal.

Brady is completely shocked by her screaming; he never saw her so mad before and he was the cause of it. His tears are a mixture of hurt and guilt as he storms out, angrily wiping them away.

Trini follows him into the hallway.

"Brady, stop!" Her face was also covered in tears. "Why would you hurt the one person who will love you unconditionally? You know how big her heart is. She may be pissed right now but she loves you, she's always loved you!" She stared him down in hurt and anger.

"You honestly believe I wanted this?! I didn't have a choice, Trini! Do you know how heartbreaking it is to be mere inches to the one you love and unable to touch her? Her scent drives me to the brink of insanity, it is the most intoxicating scent to ever grace my nose. I never wanted to deny her those tingles and sparks she was so desperately looking for. All I wanted was to tell her I love her and want nothing more than to hear her say that she loves me too. I haven't been lying for two years. I've been tortured, utterly TORTURED! And now...she hates me...all I wanted was to keep her safe. I can't deal with this; I need to get out of here." And he takes off.

With her head spinning at everything he confessed, she gathers herself and goes back inside.

"Den you need to go be with him, he is really torn up."

"But she's my sister, I need to be here for her too." Trini takes his hand in hers. "Don't worry I got her plus your uncles are right outside. Go, he shouldn't be alone, not after what he just told me."

Curious by her last statement Kamden heads to the falls, it never fails as Brady's go to place when he feels lost.

Sure enough there Brady was, sitting on a tree stump with his head down and in a dark place. Den tries to approach him cautiously but with his wolf hearing at an all-time high due to the stressful situation, he knew Den was there 500 feet ago.

Before Den could utter a syllable, Brady spoke up, "I love her Den, so much. My entire life revolves around Riri! Her touch, her radiant smile, even when she rags on me. Every day I get to see her is the best day of my life. She's perfect and she's mine but my mother...excuse me, Carolyn..." He trails off as he stares at the water cascading over the falls edge.

"I put her in danger and look what happened, what if that was actual poison? I would have lost her. I need to stop Carolyn, I have to. The woman I knew is dead, this demon is not my mother."

Den hugs him tight, Brady had gone through so much, revealed so much. His head was swirling with so many thoughts. Would Den push him away too? End their friendship? Or even have him locked up for endangering his sister and lying?

After a few more moments of silence Den sighs, "So you're my sister's mate...thank the Moon Goddess!" Brady looks at him suspiciously and he explains. "I know it looks bleak right now, but my sister will forgive you once you tell her everything and I do mean everything. I'm glad it's you and not some cocky asshole, like that jackass Roman Rivers, I hate that guy." They both laugh loudly "So I guess that makes you our Luna, right?!"

Brady punches Den in his arm and Den yelps, rubbing the bruise.

"Ha ha but for real Den, I'll do anything to make this right with her. She was just so angry with me, I disappointed her, I let her down, man. I'm a terrible mate."

He claps him on the back, "You're not a bad mate, you've been under pressure for so long and trying to do this alone but now you don't have to, you have us and we're family, quite literally now. So, let's hatch a plan to get you out of this, keep our pack safe, and get your girl back."

Den was beyond shocked when Brady revealed all the gory details.

The worst was yet to come when Den had to call his parents on their overdue vacation to reveal the diagnosis. They will blow a gasket, especially his mother.

After nearly two decades of peace, her troubles had rolled over in their grave to threaten her children and if you hadn't known before, Kamari Lee Miller was not one to mess with, especially when it came to her children.

Den makes the toughest call of his life.

"Hi...hi dad, mom, how was the flight?"

"It was okay, Den, how is your sister? What did the doctor say, is she alright?"

He clears his throat. "Well, it wasn't poison but an elixir to keep her from finding her mate." He explains it all to his parents, and he could hear his father steadily trying to calm Kam down, well...not Kam but Penelope...

"Penelope, honey please, calm down..."

Her purple hair twisted between her fingers as she tries to think of all the ways to torture those who mean to harm her kids. She had learned to control her powers, but it wasn't easy for this particular situation.

"You have got to be fucking kidding me! They poison our daughter in hopes to keep her from her mate and why, so she doesn't receive her powers and that doesn't sound like a good damn reason to be pissed? Get. Me. Home. NOW, Kayden James!"

Kayd sighs defeatedly into the phone. "We'll be home soon son, just keep her safe." With that, he ends the call to deal with his irate wife's witch alter ego. She had every right to be, these were her children and you do not mess with a mama bear's cubs.

"Penelope, please! I swear we're leaving right now but I don't feel safe with you so angry. What if lightning strikes the jet? You know what happened when you lost control last time with, well you know. We will deal with this when we get home, I promise you."

Her hair reverts to her beautiful curls, she blinks, and her hazel-green eyes are back but she is still pissed, grinding her teeth. He goes for her hands, but she flinches.

"DON'T, just get us home now." She shakes her head as the pilot starts the engines. Kayd observes his wife until the angry tears begin to fall, he unbuckles from his seat and kneels in front of her.

"Don't cry, baby. We will fix this, we won't let them win, I promise you."

She puts her hands in his. "I can't believe I'm still being tortured by those two...I'm so tired of fighting, just so tired."

"I know baby, I know, why don't you go lie down and I'll come in after I get a report from Brent. I swear I will make everything right." She nods, too overcome with emotion and worry.

Kayd: Brent, where is everyone?

B: The kids are all here, but Brady is out in the hallway, he looks like he's in a bad way. When we came to the room, he had stormed out in tears with Trinity behind him.

Kayd: We have an old situation reemerging and you will not believe me when I tell you...

He begins to break down the situation from what his son told him.

B: Dude, this is total insanity, are you kidding me?! Ugh....there goes my relaxing retirement. I'll relay the info and we'll meet in your old office in the morning.

Kayd: Thank you, I will not allow this shit to happen again especially with my baby girl. Let their whole family show up. I will gladly rip their throats out one by one!

Kayd's eyes flicker, Phoenix was scratching at the surface trying to take over.

P: I want their blood for hurting my daughter! I want to see them take their last breath after I mutilate them beyond recognition! This is a war, and I will burn them all to the ground!

Kayd inhales and exhales sharply trying to gain some control back. He goes into the bedroom and wraps his arms around her. She is still sniffling, but she turns around to meet his gaze, her eyes full of tears.

"I don't want anything to happen to my kids, they're all I have, baby." He doesn't say a word, just squeezes her tighter.

"I know you're out there, Brady Marshall Preston!"

He flinches at the use of his whole name, as Evan pats his back in reassurance or pity, he wasn't quite sure.

"Honesty is the best policy, she'll understand but you have to trust her. Now go...that family's anger issues border insanity."

He stands tall as he opens her hospital room door. When he saw her, it finally hit, the raw emotion, two years of adoration, love, passion is all he felt at just the sight of her. She was absolutely beautiful, and she was his. Her scent is stronger.

He lets out a low growl. "Mine, all mine."

Enthralled by every feature of her, his eyes turned pitch black, Raven had taken over.

"Raven sorry stupid human took pills, he listened to mom who didn't love him. No excuse, we make up to mate for a lifetime." He nuzzles her hand, purring like a kitten.

She sniffles then laughs, "I have been waiting for someone to tell me that I was theirs and sadly I don't feel a thing..."

Raven stumbles back looking at her so heartbroken, giving Brady a chance to regain control.

"Raven, oh gosh! Brady, tell him I didn't mean it like that. I mean because of the drugging."

He tried to talk to Raven but he was lying in the fetal position with his ears drawn back, he shut off his link.

Brady shakes his head, "Just give him some time, he was constantly telling me that this wasn't a good idea, but I just wanted my mom back and I was willing to do anything until I realized that she wasn't my mother, she is evil and malicious, my mother is dead."

He takes her hands and laughs as he finally feels the tingles and sparks but his face falls when she doesn't react the same or at all. He puts his head in her lap. She strokes his hair.

"I'm glad to see you feeling what I've been yearning for, do you get it now? No more lies Brady. I will never think less of you, you're my mate but you were my friend first."

He spends the rest of the night telling her every single detail until they fall asleep in each other's arms in her bed with him kissing her forehead throughout the night into early morning. He relished in her touch; her beauty magnified seeing her with his senses intact.

Tomorrow, they will gather to plan for an all-out war...

Love Changes Everything

He couldn't get enough of her touch, it felt like a million tiny explosions throughout his body.

"I can't believe I denied myself this feeling for so long. Can you ever forgive me?" His fingers release hers sliding down her arm and back.

"I told you I forgive you for the millionth time last night! It's not your fault if it were me, I'd do the same, our mothers are everything to us. Luckily, you have Ms. Gracie who's been a much better mother to you. What a turn of events! I have to be honest; my parents are going to probably be livid that we didn't know you were related to the infamous Bridget."

He kisses her hand. "I know and I hope your mother doesn't rip me in half, this could be our first and last day together."

She turns to face him, and he looks genuinely worried, it wasn't until his mother's confession of her evil plan did he know he was related to Bridget. He never thought about his mother's maiden name. It was a black mark on the family.

"Don't worry, I will talk to her. She wouldn't take you from me."

He runs his fingers through her curls. "Still, if they object, I have to respect their wishes. My family has caused enough problems already."

She sits up and looks down at him, eyeing him suspiciously. "If you're even considering not being by my side you can shut up right now. Just because I can't feel our connection right now doesn't give you the right to hurt my feelings! Two years I've waited, two long years to find the love of my life and here you are, I love you, are you really going to look me in the eye and say you wouldn't do anything to be with me? Tell me right now or I swear I will walk out and not look back!"

She was tired and frustrated and all she wanted was to feel the mate bond and be happy...

"Y-you love me?"

She sighs, "Don't change the subject, Brady..."

He sits up looking her in her eyes. There was a spark there trying to work its way through the drugs. "I'm not changing the subject, you clearly said it. Say it again, please baby, I need to hear you." And for the first time, he leans over, and his lips meet hers. He sits back gauging her reaction.

Her fingers touch her own lips as she takes in what just happened and her heart melts all over again. "I do love you, Brady, even before I knew what this was." He kisses her again over and over.

He couldn't stop smiling. "I've been waiting forever to say this. Kayari Denise Miller, my Riri, I love you, too."

They didn't even realize that her brother, best friend, and uncles were all in the room.

"I'd say get a room but sadly we're in it."

Den hugs her, "I'm happy for you my sweet and annoying sister. And you know, typical sibling threat to murder you if you do anything to hurt her." Brady just nods in agreement.

Trini squeals loud enough to wake the dead. "Finally! I'm so happy for you! Wait, so does that mean he's our Luna too? What do you call a male Luna anyway, a Lune?"

Brady groans as she brings up the same subject that Den so said yesterday. "I'm just the Beta and mate to a beautiful Alpha female, no additional titles needed."

She pouts at him, "No pet names?"

He snuggles into her, inhaling her. "You, baby, can call me whatever you want."

Evan clears his throat. "I'm happy for you but your parents are on their way and I'm unsure how they will react to your mate being related to their sworn enemy.

We need to be levelheaded and realize their reaction is based on fear and not because they hate you, Brady. If anything, your mother is to blame."

Just then the door opened and there was the one person who didn't know that Carolyn was alive...his father. A look of pure shock was on his face as Gracie tried to absorb the news as well.

"Is it true, son?" His father's face had fallen, and tears were forming as Gracie squeezed his hand to comfort him. "S-she's alive? Your mother is alive?"

He pulls away and steps toward his son who is standing next to Kay's bed.

Brady was hesitant, scared to answer. His body language spoke volumes when he couldn't.

How does he explain how he knew for over two years his mother was alive?

He could feel all the anger and hatred boil up to the surface and was not going to filter his true feelings.

"That vindictive bitch is not my mother! She used me to exact her revenge for Aunt Bridget, but we all know she deserved to die! She deserved her slow and painful death and I wish I were there to watch her burn! Carolyn lied to me, she used me, she threatened to kill my mate if I didn't do what she said, I couldn't let that happen, I--I love her. I'm sorry I lied Dad, lied to you all this time but that mom, our mom, is gone, she died the minute she told me she didn't care or love us that her revenge was more important or when she decided to shack up with that bastard. She's a rogue, she's a rogue's whore! SHE. IS. NOT. MY. MOTHER!"

Brady drops to his knees as he drains all emotion over her. He was panting, exhausted, and overwhelmed. "She's...not my mother...Gracie is, she loves me as a mother should." His father collapses over his son wrapping him in his arms.

"Sshhh, it's okay, I understand. You're right she is not the woman I was once in love with but to pit her son against his friends and hide it from me...I just can't believe who she has become, she is a monster. Let's go home and talk, you'll need to explain to her parents everything. This is war and Carolyn's willingness to destroy us all in the name of her sister." He helps him up, but he doesn't leave her side.

Family Plan

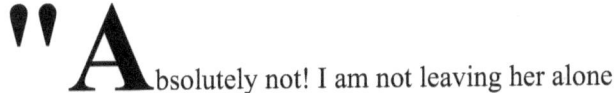

"**A**bsolutely not! I am not leaving her alone.

They got to her when she was out of my sight for a few minutes, I will not allow them that close again."

"Brady, I'm fine, my uncles and my brother are here, besides, I've been released to go home. I'll be right there when you get back. I want you, umm, I want you to..."

She looks around, hesitant to say it out loud.

He squeezes her hand for reassurance. "Look at me. Tell me..."

She places her hand on his face and he leans into it, inhaling her scent. "Stay with me..."

The staff at the house were moving their parents into a townhouse not too far from the main house and the children were moving from their rooms to a modified set up. Their parents' room and their old nursery were reconstructed turning them into King and Queen style suites. She wanted Brady to move into the big house and her room, she knew they wouldn't be able to be away from each other for too long.

He kisses her forehead then her hand, "Absolutely, I will bring some things by after I talk with my parents. Save me a spot...in *our* bed, baby girl." She agrees and he leaves with his parents, blowing her a final kiss.

She sighs heavily, getting out of bed to change to go home. "Hey Den, can you make sure I have everything, the sooner we leave this place the better."

She looked at her reflection in the mirror, she was a mess in a plain white tee and black basketball shorts her brother brought because that dress was far too binding, she did look amazing though, as she thought back. She grimaces at the state of her curls and her makeup, she looked tragic but the one thing that made it okay is that he saw through all that, he saw her as beautiful anyway. Still, she couldn't wait to go home to shower and feel like herself again. She couldn't wait to feel what he felt the moment he touched her.

She touches her lips once again reflecting on their first kiss. Her lips tugged into a smile as she whispered "Mine."

"You want me to do WHAT?! Are you insane?! I just felt everything today, the sparks, the tingles, the butterflies in my stomach, pure unadulterated love, and now you want me to take those horrible pills again?" He stares flabbergasted at his parents and hers as well. They were waiting for them at their house needing an explanation before they needed a shower.

"Forgive me Alpha and Luna but that is crazy! My mom knows I stopped taking them you don't think she'll be a little suspicious when I start taking them again on my own free will? She'll smell that a mile away. We need to attack her before she attacks my baby again, I cannot lose her!"

Kam's heart softens, it was like watching her life all over again. When she looks back how could it have not been any clearer that it was Brady? He was head over heels in love with her daughter, but he never seemed to cross that friendship line and she never knew why until he explained the entire situation. What a horrible excuse for a mother, she thought. She couldn't even fathom how she could abandon her family in the name of revenge, for a woman who would endanger someone pregnant, who would run after a slob who didn't even fit the description of a man. The thoughts made her queasy, even from beyond the grave *she* was still the bane of her existence.

"Excuse me, I just need to get some air." She quickly steps outside to the back porch and sits on the swing with her head down.

She heard the door close. "Are you okay, baby doll?"

She shakes her head. "Just the thought of everything makes me physically sick. I will not let this affect my baby girl, not a chance in hell. We end this and we do it soon, Kayd. Penelope is keeping radio silence again; she is preparing for a war and I am not fighting her on this one. She's going to decimate every enemy in her path...and I am going to let her, fair warning."

He knew Penelope's radio silence was code for she was about to rain hell on those who hurt her family. She had become familiar with more dark spells, for all he knew she was learning more as they spoke. She leans into him as he wraps his arms around her, "We just need a plan, we can't go blind because that's how mistakes are made." They sit out there for a few more minutes before heading back inside the house to brainstorm.

They assure Brady that there are no hard feelings towards him and that they were excited to have him as their daughter's mate. It felt like a ton of bricks lifted as Kayd hugged him and Kam kissed his cheek. All he wanted was their acceptance and now he had it. For that, he would battle to the death to keep Kay safe, but for now, it was time for him to go home.

Home...to her.

Coming Home

Kay looks around at her new suite set up. She had

picked burgundy, black, and gold to decorate her room. Her poster bed was center stage on a platform with burgundy and gold fabric wrapped around the posts. She had a lounge area near her window with two chairs and a small bistro-style table.

Her favorite area was a reading nook where there were bookcases embedded in the wall, opposite the window, and already filled to the brim with classics from Tolstoy to Dickens to Shakespeare. Her walk-in closet was slightly larger and displayed all her clothing, she had only used one side of the massive closet the other side was for him. Her bathroom was modeled after her old one, but the colors were changed to a deep navy and sea green. She chose more gender-neutral colors knowing that eventually she would be sharing her space and that moment came sooner than she thought. She makes sure she has everything they will need for their room; she had a pack member run to the store for all the essentials.

After all that she showers and settles into bed finding a movie to watch as she waits for her mate to come home.

Home...

He was coming home to her.

The past 24 hours had been exhausting, but she smiled as she nodded off to sleep.

Brent was standing guard when Den, Trini, and Brady walked up the stairs.

Den was excited to see his remodeled room; he chose a basketball theme. He pulls Trini with him and she tells Brady to tell Kay to text when she is ready for visitors.

He stands in front of the door with his overnight bag and smiles to himself.

Brent states that her security detail will be here in twenty minutes as he heads downstairs.

The twins had assigned guards when their parents needed them protected. Xavier and Knox led her team, they were the two largest wolves you have ever seen. Xavier was at least six foot nine and Knox was about six foot seven, they radiated intimidation in their black suits and shades and if that didn't work, they always had those large gun-shaped lumps in their jacket pockets.

Brady touches the mahogany door before knocking lightly. He opens the door to find her snuggled in her pillows, halfway tossed out of her blanket. She had showered and changed into her grey sweat shorts and a burgundy crop top; her hair pulled into a loose ponytail.

He couldn't believe how gorgeous she was. Kay wasn't one of those girls who needed makeup or even used it unless Trini applied it, she had a natural beauty that needed no enhancement. He set down his bag on what he assumed was his side of the bed and removed his t-shirt, shoes, and socks leaving only his black sweatpants on. He slips in and pulls her to his chest; it was only then that she started to stir.

"Oh Michael, go away, we can't be seen together anymore my mate might catch us... I'll miss our fun little romps in bed, though."

He growls, "Who the hell is Michael?!"

She bursts out laughing and pinches his face to calm him down.

"Oh my gosh, you should have seen your face! Hahahaha! Just because we're mates doesn't mean I won't still poke fun. You're adorable when you're jealous."

He squeezes her sides making her jump and squeal. "You think that's funny? I'll get you back, just you wait." She wraps her arms around tighter as he kisses her forehead, settling into the bed.

After a few moments of silence, he looks down at her, "Hi."

"Hi...I missed you."

"I missed you so much more! Oh, Trini said whenever you're ready for a visit to text her, she's in Den's room."

She shakes her head, "No, I just want to be here with you, just us."

She's reluctant to broach the subject but she must, "So my parents didn't kill you, that's a good sign, right?"

"Right."

"So, did you guys come up with a plan?"

He shakes his head. "Not yet, but we'll worry about that tomorrow, I just want to be in the moment with you, baby girl."

She blushes, "Sounds like a great plan." Then she bolts upright. "Trini!" She's frantically looking for something.

"What? What is it?" She pulls the covers and leans over the bed forgetting she was in shorts; the sight drives him crazy as he growls.

"Tonight! Tonight is Trini's date with my brother. I said I would help." She finally discovers her phone underneath her pillow.

Kay: OMG I almost forgot your date with my brother!

T: You don't have to help. I know you want to bond with your mate.

Kay: No, besides, it won't take long because my best friend is already soooo gorgeous! Come by in ten...

T: Okay! BTW...Eeeeeeeee!

She can basically hear her inner eardrums burst. She sits up to slide out of bed but not before he drags her back. She turns to see a pout on his face.

"Don't you guilt trip me, I promised to help, and I've been waiting for them to get together since forever." He kisses her shoulder.

"I'm sure they said the same about us. Well, can I stay and watch? I don't want you out of my sight for a single second." She bites her lip and he sighs heavily.

He pulls her lip free, "I know you can't feel anything, but I definitely can and that...is not helping." He lets out a lustful growl as she blushes.

"Of course you can stay, it's our room. That's still so weird to say! You're my mate...I never would have guessed it was you. I thought you thought of me as a bratty little sister."

He shakes his head. "Not a chance, especially with the thoughts I had about you every night."

She was shocked. They hadn't talked about the mating process and the fact she was still a virgin, she wondered if he was too or if he let carnal temptation win. Just the idea he kissed someone else hurt like hell. She sighed;

her expression changed to worry at the thought of him being with someone else. Her heart sank and her thoughts ran wild, she started to withdraw from him.

He noticed her mood change right away, "Hey, what's wrong?" She shakes her head and walks into the bathroom with a simple "nothing" and closes the door.

Date Night with My Brother

Five minutes later she heard Trini knock on their door and a second later a knock on the bathroom before she barges in.

"You know I never kno--"

She stops when she sees Kay in worried thought, biting the inside of her cheeks, tears threatening to shed.

She looks up and Trini speaks up, "Hey."

And the dam burst. Kay chokes on her sobs, she couldn't hold them anymore.

Trini wraps her in her arms. "Hey hey hey, what's going on?"

She blurts out, "I'm a virgin!"

Trinity laughs a bit, "Uhh, I know that, so what?"

She sniffles, wiping her tears. "But what if he isn't? I would be heartbroken if he had sex with another girl all the while he was hiding his scent from me."

"Sorry to say but the wolves of our generation don't hold to those standards that our parents did anymore so you may have to accept the fact that he may have been with someone else, but Brady's a good guy and he adores you."

She snorts, "He spends time with the proverbial manwhore himself, I'm sure he's had plenty of chances. Look at him, he's gorgeous and every girl wanted him, I'm sure they still do. And me, I wouldn't even know what to do! I don't want to disappoint him."

Trini could see the wheels turning on a subject that didn't need that depth of thought.

"Stop it, right now. You are everything he could ever want! This conversation is ridiculous! Yes, you are a virgin and that's okay. You set your standards high and that's what makes you a prize catch. So, don't downplay your decision, you did that for you, and I can say I'm glad you did. I'll never forget my first time with Bailey Evergreen, he was terrible, I could fry an egg and it would take longer than he did." They burst out laughing.

"Be proud to be you, Kay. He loves you and if you have a concern just ask, I'm sure he'd have no problem telling you...now, let's focus on the task at hand, getting your manwhore brother's jaw to drop at the sight of me."

She sighs, "I'm sorry I shouldn't have used that word to describe him."

Trini shrugs, "Hey, that just means my chances for success increase." She winks and Kay pretends to gag.

Once her makeup is complete, they tiptoe to her closet as Brady sleeps. He was lying on his back, one hand behind his head and one leg bent at the knee.

In her closet, she is going through her options when Trini looks back at Brady again.

"Hot damn girl! I can't believe you left that sexiness there to help me, if it were me..." Kay lets a growl slip then covers her mouth in shock.

"I'm sorry, I didn't even know I was going to do that!"

Trini smiles widely as she jumps up. "Ooh, someone's getting territorial! The drugs must be working their way out of your system faster than expected or maybe it's your Legacy powers!"

She looks at him and smiles, "I hope so. Okay, so is that the dress you want to wear because I have a pair of leopard print heels that would go perfectly, they're over there, top left shoebox." Her best friend goes to shower and change.

Kay wanders to bed and sits on the edge staring at him. He looked so peaceful...so gorg...

"You know... I'd find this rather creepy if you weren't my dream girl..." His eyes open to catch her blushing.

His arms wrap around so quickly, and she couldn't help but giggle.

"Stoooop, Trini's in the bathroom getting ready! Brady..."

He ignores her pleas and places gentle kisses from nape to shoulder. "You're driving me wild; Raven is trying so hard to take over, I don't know how long I can last with you in my arms so close to me, your scent is addictive." His reins of control were slipping.

R: Silly human, take her now! She's ours and I want her!

B: Who's in charge here? Besides, she's still drugged. I want her reaction to be genuine and as full of raw passion as mine is. That time is supposed to be special.

R: YOU WERE EAVESDROPPING!

Feeling caught, he couldn't deny it.

B: She pulled away from me, I knew something was wrong, but I wouldn't have suspected that.

R: Well, buddy, you better say something because she's looking dead at you, right now."

Raven skips off somewhere deep into his subconscious.

"Stupid mutt." He huffs.

"Did you drift off while I was talking to you?"

For a second, he takes in all the features of her face from her smooth silky skin to her gorgeous green eyes with the hazel border, her perfect smile and her eyebrows knitted waiting for his response. He snaps out of his trance.

"Oh, yeah Raven was arguing with me."

R: LIAR!

He skips away again. He rolls his eyes at the nerve of his very own wolf.

"Anyway, Kay we need to talk...I have to be honest I heard..."

The Next Morning

Her bathroom door flies open and Trini models

the little black dress and leopard heels.

"Well? What do you think? You think he'll like it?" She
is desperately hoping for the right answer, this was the
date she had been waiting for. Kay walks up and hugs
her, taking her hands.

"Wow, he is going to go absolutely nuts for you. You are
stunning, now, go...have fun with my brother and for the
love of Moon Goddess DO NOT TELL ME!" Kay
embraces her best friend and whispers "I'm so happy you
guys are giving this a chance."

To which she replies, "Don't forget to tell him, he's
going to sense something wrong. Tell him, he loves
you." She nods as her friend closes the door.

She inhales deeply and exhales turning around.
"Sweetheart, we need to talk..."

He shrugs his shoulders "I already said that remember? I
was saying something before Trini came out?"

She does remember and climbs into bed sitting like a child while he is laying on his side, his weight perched on his elbow.

"What I was going to say was that I heard your conversation. Something was bothering you and I knew you'd tell your best friend. I'm sorry I eavesdropped but I was concerned."

"And now?"

He smiles, takes her hand and begins to chuckle. "You have absolutely nothing to worry about, although I hang out with your brother, I have never slept with anyone, I was serious when I told you that guys look for their soulmates, too. And that girl, whatever her name is, was just so...pushy..."

"The word you are looking for is slutty but go on..."

"Yeah that, but the moment I saw the disappointment on your face I had to make it right. When she touched me, it felt so wrong, so off."

She takes him by surprise by straddling his lap and he groans. "Sweetheart... I am only so strong." She settles further into his lap causing his own hands to smack his face as he growls this time.

"Mmm, so you're telling me you're a virgin?" She rocks back and forth. The motion is quite triggering as he moans loudly.

"Riri, baby, please..." She slows her motions.

"Just answer the question and I might stop torturing you."

He grabs her hips and flips them so that he is on top. His lips just inches from hers as he teases and tortures her. Just a hair from a kiss he smiles wide, "Yes, my first time will be with you and only you."

He gives her a quick peck as torture before laying on his side again. She is beaming at the news. "So, when do we, you know?"

He's shocked by the question. "I don't think we schedule it or anything, we just let it happen but not until those drugs are completely out of your system. I want you to feel everything. Every touch of me all over you, every kiss, and I want to hear every whimper, cry, and moan from our first time." She whines as his kisses trail from her lips to her stomach and he comes back up to hold her.

They lay in silence until they fall asleep.

The next morning Kay wakes up to emptiness, she looks around for signs he was still in the room but heard nothing, but a delicious smell wafted into the bedroom, it was pancakes and bacon. She stretches, brushes her teeth, and adjusts her hair before heading downstairs. As she was heading towards the kitchen, she could hear the utensils clinking against the cookware. Before she could turn into the kitchen, she heard a female voice.

"Morning Brady, how sweet of you to make me breakfast..." He looks over his shoulder with a look of amusement as he rolls his eyes and turns back to the stove. She steps from behind the island counter gradually getting closer. A surge of anger rose in Kay that she hadn't felt before. She only thought of ripping her throat out and discarding her in the recycle bin.

"Contrary to your belief Lauren, this isn't for you. You'll have to find your own meal." He plates a couple of pancakes before placing the pan back on the fire to get ready for another set.

"Oh, that's okay. I'm looking at the meal I want right now. You ran off before we could schedule our little meetup." She neglected to correct him on her name. She was too busy inching closer and closer until her chest was inches from his back.

"I think you should take your flirting elsewhere, I told you I wasn't interested, Lily."

She huffs and stands directly in front between him and the stove.

"It's Melody! Now, how about we go somewhere where I can make you remember my name? I can even have you scream it..." She bites her lip and that was it, he needed to shut this down.

"Look, I don't care what your name is, I have my mate." He tries to gain some space between them, but she just moves closer.

She sniffs him and grins, "Oh...the pack princess is your mate, how...cute but you haven't claimed her yet so you're still fair game. Come on, she'll never know, and you might enjoy it."

Before Melody could even blink, she found herself slammed hard on the kitchen island with a highly irate Kay baring her teeth and growling, her Alpha dominance undeniable. Her eyes pitch black in anger, Duchess had taken over and she was about to send her a clear message to back the fuck off.

"You just can't seem to stay away from what's ours, first our father and now our mate? Listen closely and carefully, *Melody*, leave Brady alone or I swear I will dismember every last inch of you, there won't be enough of a body to claim. It is taking every last fiber in me not to have a little snack, but Kay would not be too happy with me so I will leave you with this; walk away now before I ban you from this pack and leave you to be the rogue whore you were meant to be. Touch what's mine again and you're dead."

Melody looks shocked by her actions. She grabs her neck trying to catch her breath and backs away slowly without another syllable.

Going for a Run

"**W**hoa!"

Was all he could muster after seeing that. Kay had gained control back and was breathing hard as she gripped the countertop in an effort to calm Duchess down, she was still growling in rage.

He places his hands on her shoulders to comfort her and she jumps immediately when she feels the sparks, the tingles. She gasps and turns around. She takes his hands and closes her eyes, a smile plastered on her face. He felt it as well, but it was stronger and seemed to be coursing from her body to his in an endless loop.

"I-I can feel it, the sparks! The meds wore off. They finally wore off! It's...beautiful." She starts to cry and he's just smiling at her reaction.

"You're so beautiful when you're happy. But how is this even possible? The doctor said it would take up to a week?"

"For normal wolves but I'm also a Legacy, maybe that had something to do with it. Who cares?! Baby, I can feel it, I've dreamt of this moment for years and it's finally..." She gets choked up and he hugs her further intensifying the explosions going on between them. He kisses the top of her head as Den and Trini walk in.

"What's going on?"

Kay sniffles and wipes the tears from her face, she notices Trini in Den's favorite basketball tee. She smiles at her best friend who understood the unspoken conversation. They both merely nod at each other.

"The meds wore off and she can fully feel our mate bond now." He kisses her forehead and she smiles squeezing his waist. "I just realized, were you making breakfast for me?"

"Oh, you mean before you body slammed what's her name onto the kitchen countertop?"

"She was flirting with what's mine; I was sick of her anyway. Bet I made my point crystal clear." He leans down to meet her lips in a sweet kiss. "You absolutely did, baby."

Kamden and Trinity both look confused, "Don't worry, you had to be there." They laugh as he puts their plates down on the breakfast nook while Den prepares an omelet for him and Trini.

Brady pours the orange juice before sitting down, placing a quick kiss to her lips.

"You just can't stop, can you?"

He shakes his head, "Nope. Raven is jumping for joy that you're fine now. He's asking about...well, you know."

Her cheeks instantly go red and she shakes her head. "We'll talk about all that later, I promise."

After breakfast, Kay takes a shower and puts on her black crop leggings and a green sports bra covering it in a t-shirt crop top. She was going for a much-needed run to the falls and back. She pulls her hair up and heads out, much to Brady's dismay. She swore she'd be back in twenty and if she were a second late, he could come looking for her. Since her dad had been working to prepare them, she had gotten used to running every day and so she couldn't slack off just because she had been in the hospital. She was an Alpha female and a Legacy; she would work through the pain and exhaustion.

She found herself a bit winded quicker than usual, she took a quick break. She could hear the falls but decided not to push too hard and stood against a tree. "Jeez, one day and I already can't make the trip to the falls, how sad is...mmm!"

A clothed hand went over her mouth and before she could fight back darkness had taken over.

"Hey Den, I--"

Brady starts sniffing around as they head towards the door with their friends Paul and Jessie behind them. He is constantly sniffing as if looking for something.

Before he could reach the door, he collapsed in excruciating pain.

"Fuck! AHHH!"

Tears immediately sprung from the sharp pains jabbing him in the abdomen, but it wasn't just that...

"Brady, talk to me, what's happening?!"

"So-something happened I felt a pain in my neck and now I-I can't smell her scent anymore. I can't sense her, something is wrong! The scent is gone again. Den, she's got her! My bitch mother got her! I need to find her!"

And like that, Brady shifts and is following her scent as far as he possibly could. She was on her way to the falls; he remembers her telling him that. He knew he shouldn't have let her go alone but she insisted she was fine. He should have known that as long as Carolyn was in the shadows, she wasn't safe.

He panicked at all the things his "mother" could be doing to her right now.

He shifted gears towards Alpha Damien's house with rage in his eyes. He linked Den and told him where he was headed. When he shifted back, he could see his mother happily tending to the kitchen, she seemed content being a rogue's whore but that was not his concern. He kicks the patio door that leads into the kitchen down with a thunderous roar.

Alpha Damien stands to confront but by the fury on Brady's face, he second guesses his next course of action. Teeth bared Brady steps into the kitchen.

"You have two seconds to tell me where she is before I kill you where you stand and don't get it twisted, Carolyn, I'd rip you to shreds for simply breathing, now, where is she?!"

She looks at her irate son and scoffs before continuing washing dishes, "I don't know what you are talking about, if you're talking about your precious little mate we don't have her, maybe somebody did our dirty work for us and rid the world of that spoiled bit--"

She can't breathe with his claws wrapped around her throat, squeezing tighter and tighter. At this moment Raven had taken control and did not contemplate killing her now, but he may not get any answers if they did have her.

His pitch-black eyes pierced her soul, "I will not warn you again, Carolyn, watch what you say about my wife."

She laughs even though she barely has any wind to take a decent breath.

"Already claiming her are we, how do you even know she'll last long enough to see the day? There's nothing I want more than the demise of that wretched family and if my son has to suffer in the aftermath then so be it."

Raven's rage was boiling over at the thought of losing Kay by her hands, he would not have it. He squeezes tighter and she struggles for the tiniest bit of air.

"That's right, you don't care because if you did you would have dropped this revenge plot long ago, but you don't, you'll always be this vindictive witch seeking revenge for her whore of a sister!"

He drops her to a crumpled mass on the floor and sneers at Alpha Damien, slowly stalking towards him.

"And you...you're NO fucking Alpha you're just as responsible as she is and if something happened to Kay I will come back, dismantle your bodies and burn this place to the fucking ground! If you are responsible, I suggest you run...run now and run fast because I'll be coming for you and I will not hesitate to let my pack tear your pathetic followers limb from limb, but you...I'll take care of you my damn self!"

He roars loudly as he backs away from them and out the house linking anyone in the pack to see if they found any clues.

Find Her!

With no update over link, he heads back to the

pack-house where he sees a worried Kam and a violently angry Kayd.

Before he could utter a word Kayd had Brady slammed up against the wall. "Oof!"

Kam screams, "Kayd, Phoenix, please! Put Brady down, he's not responsible!" Kam's eyes glow violet as she tries to reel in Penelope, her husband, and his irate wolf.

Phoenix squeezes his grip on his throat. "Your mother's family is the bane of my existence, why would I want you messing up mine?! You better hope not a hair is harmed on our baby girl or I will personally rip your heart out and it'll be the last thing you see!"

Kam is still pleading for him to put Brady down while his eyes have returned to his natural green hue.

It breaks Brady's heart to see those green eyes that aren't hers. His heart ached as the tears broke the barrier to fall.

"I'M SORRY! I'm so so sorry...I failed her, I failed you. I never meant for this to happen. I've loved her for two years and I just got her into my arms. We shared the sparks and it...it was the best feeling ever! I would easily sacrifice my life for hers! I love her, Mr. Miller, s-so much."

Brady stops struggling, giving up on everything. He collapses into a heap on the floor in tears. He was so lost. He didn't know who had her or why or if she was even alive.

Kamden embraced his friend; he was in tears still trying to comfort his brother.

"I promise you she's okay, Brady, she's strong even stronger than her knuckleheaded brother. We're going to find her. Come on, you should lie down."

He wrenches away from Den. "I will not sleep until I find her, she's my life! My world revolves around her, I'm nothing without her. I can't..." His chest was heaving with tears pouring out of his eyes.

Kayd surprises Brady by hugging him tightly. "I know son, I know. I wouldn't trust her with anyone else. I'm sorry I overreacted, you're a good kid, I know that. I'd be proud to call you son. Let's go to the office, we can review the cameras while the border patrol scans the grounds for clues. Come on..."

In the office they review the cameras closest to the falls, there were several different angles.

"There! She took a moment to rest against that tree and then...look, somebody came behind her in all black with a towel. They drugged her. They went west near the unclaimed territory between us...and the Black Rabbit Pack."

Kam sighs, "That's 27 miles of unclaimed territory, how will we even know where to begin looking?" She looks at her husband worried, the stress of the situation dulling her beautiful face. He pulls her to him, their foreheads touching before giving her a gentle kiss.

He sighs, "Get Alpha Brenner on the phone."

A

lpha Brenner Lyons was a treacherous leader to the Black Rabbits, he was vicious and borderline cruel, but Kayden kept an open line of communication knowing that one day one of them would need the other's services.

"*Former* Alpha Miller, how can I be of service to you today?" His tone was dripping in belittlement.

Kayden swallowed the huge pill called his dignity. "Alpha Brenner I have a situation that is a very dire situation. My daughter was taken from my land and according to our surveillance, they were headed towards the direction of your land with the unchartered territory in between. Have you had any rogue activity or seen anything? Please, she's my baby girl." His heart and voice break simultaneously as he pleads with the cold-hearted Alpha.

"Alpha Miller we are not friends or even social, when we attend the same meetings, we don't even speak so why would I do you a favor such as scanning my security cameras for your precious little daughter, maybe she wasn't ready for the responsibility of being an Alpha, you know what they say about women..."

A growl slips from Kayd's lips, "Watch your very next words, Alpha, for they may be your last. I am merely asking you out of the kindness of your heart to run a security scan and report to find my daughter. Please...I am at your mercy..." Kayd chokes back the tears as he lowers his pride.

There was a long pause, the tension in the air was thick, almost suffocating. With a heavy sigh, "Very well, I will have my security review the tapes of the past two hours and will call back with a report." He went silent before stating, "I hope we can come to a mutual understanding between our packs and I sincerely hope that you find your daughter."

With that, he hangs up and Kam hugs him tight. She wipes the tears that streak his face. "I can't lose her...she's my baby girl."

Kam sighs, "Yes, baby we'll get her back...I promise, just like you promised me."

Brady slides down the wall giving up all hope. "I can't just sit here while she's out there with some...perverted psychopath! I need to look!" Just then the door swings open and the captain from the security patrol comes in.

"Alpha! We think we found an abandoned shack about twelve miles north of here, there was some movement spotted from there."

That's all it took before Brady had already shifted and was out the door with Den right behind him.

Den mind links him, "Brady, slow down. Brady stop!"

They are both running towards the location of the shack. Den's white wolf is a stark contrast to Brady's auburn one, he also inherited his dad's black circle around his left eye.

Brady doesn't respond; he keeps his pace towards the unchartered territory marked by stakes and white flags.

He was determined and nothing was going to get him to stop looking for her, for the love of his life, his mate. If only she could connect with him...

"Come on, come on, come on...Brady, where are you?!" Kay thought as she was trying to mind link him. She was surrounded by darkness, there were no lights on in this tiny space which she couldn't figure out if it was a room, a building, there were no defining features. Although she was blindfolded, she could still sense the area around her, and she could see a tiny bit from the bottom of the fabric which was tied semi-tight.

She did know she wasn't on her territory as the kidnapper was running with her on his shoulder, she had faintly noticed in her haze the white flags as he crossed the border, it was her only sign to where she might be. She kept trying to link to anyone in the pack but was unable to get past her own thoughts. They had injected her twice with an unknown substance the moment they set her down in the hard-backed chair and tied her up. Not so much as a single word was uttered before they left again.

As she was struggling the door opens, "Ah ah ahh, now we wouldn't want our princess to hurt herself, now would we?"

That voice...

No, it couldn't be... She had to confirm

But why, she thought.

It didn't make sense! She needed answers and she wanted them right now.

"Take off this blindfold I want to see the sick son of a bitch who took me from my family...NOW!" She used the full volume of her Alpha voice and it shook the walls.

"Tsk tsk, now is that how a lady asks for a favor? Let's try again with some manners, now...what does my princess want?" The voice was sickeningly sweet and made her stomach turn.

She swallowed the bile creeping up her throat. "P-please..."

Soon the blindfold is yanked from her forcefully and the blinding glow now shining from above causes her to blink rapidly to adjust to the light. Her vision comes back slowly as she looks at the figure towering above but slightly behind her, brushing her hair, stroking her cheek. She flinches from the touch. He takes that motion to step into her line of sight.

"**R**oman?! What the hell are you doing? Take me back, this instant! Have you lost your mind? What is this? How--"

He slaps his hand against her mouth to stop her from talking but it also cuts off her airway. He removes it so she can breathe.

"Now, is that any way for my princess to speak to her true love, hmm?"

She laughs hysterically thinking this was all a joke. "You're kidding right, you...you have to be! Roman, we shared ONE kiss in grade school, and then you disappeared. It was innocent and didn't mean anything! This is completely insane...you're insane!"

He pushes her chair forcefully until it hits the wall causing her to gasp, her eyes wide. His face twisted in fury and rage.

"Shut up! You don't know anything! That kiss meant everything to me! Y-you don't know the pain and devastation I went through to leave you here with all those other males looking at you like they had a chance, but they didn't...you were mine the moment I saw you. We can make it work baby, live a long and happy life together. All I have to do is mark you and we can start our lives together." He bares his teeth inching closer and closer to the spot between her neck and shoulder.

"Stop! This is wrong and you c-can't...I have my mate..." He stops and looks at her, tilting his head.

"You what?"

She swallows hard, "I met my mate Roman and he's going to come looking for me. Please, just let me go. Our time together was meant to be temporary, and I enjoyed it but...I'm in love with Brady." She smiles uncontrollably causing him to act out and throw a table she didn't even know was there, shattering it to pieces causing her to yelp. She kept trying to expand the distance between them now she was shaking in fear. "S-stay away!"

His face twists into a wicked smile before he leans forward, hands resting on the arms of the chair.

"I know you're not talking about that loser from the party who took you from me. Please, he is nowhere near the caliber that I am. Oh...ha ha ha how you love to tease me. No one needs to come for you, because you were meant to be with me, don't you get it? I love you, Kay. I can't wait to have that sweet body underneath me, writhing in pain...and pleasure."

She is so close to gagging but just shakes her head, squeezing her eyes tight, still desperately trying to connect with someone, anyone.

"Try all you want, darling but I injected you with a powerful link blocker and the same stuff from your coronation. Fun stuff, huh?! Your precious "mate" can't sense you and therefore...you're all mine. Isn't that great?!" His sadistic smile drops into an emotionless grin.

"SAY. IT. Isn't it great?" He had a look of no turning back; he was teetering between rationality and insanity. She had to keep him happy until she found a way out.

"Y-yeah great, I'm so hap-happy we finally get to be together, just you...and me." She plastered a fake smile across her face.

He places his hand on her chin and tilts it up to meet his eye. Scanning her face for a sign of whether she was lying or not. He seemed content in her answer and smiled, patting her head.

"I'm so glad we came to an agreement. Now, my love, what would you like for dinner?"

Kay: For dinner? He's certifiable! Ok...just...keep calm. He's coming, my love is coming, I know it.

She could only shrug her shoulders. "I don't know, honey. You decide, please?" She puts on a front and his smile is a mile wide as he nods.

"Anything for you, sweetheart." He kisses her forehead and she refrains from flinching or gagging further. She just smirks as he heads out the door.

Once the door shuts, she screams out in frustration. "What...in the fucking hell is happening?! Please...Brady...find me."

The wind, landscape, and scenery were all going by in a blur. He could feel the emotion draining through his tear ducts, but he couldn't stop, he wouldn't. Just beyond the tree line, he could spot something structural.

B: Den, where are the others?

D: Dad said border patrol is watching our land and security is surrounding the unclaimed territory. He's back at the house just in case she returns.

B: Good because if she is there, I am going to violently murder the bastard who took her from me. There's no keeping my anger in so don't try to stop me either. I WILL be covered in their blood.

D: Are you kidding me, I want in on the torture of this sick bastard. I get it B, let's get my sister.

Kay jumps when the door opens and Roman strolls in with takeout boxes. He turns on a lone lamp, instead of the overhead light, to give the place some ambiance but to her, it just gave an even creepier vibe.

"I'm so sorry, love, that the atmosphere isn't more...romantic but I promise I'll make it up to you. We can go to the most romantic city in the world, Paris. Would you like that? We can sail down the Seine and then we'll go to the top of the Eiffel Tower and we'll dance at the rooftop restaurant basking in..."

"AHHH! Cut the bullshit, Roman! I don't want to go anywhere with you! You're crazy do you realize that?! I will NEVER EVER fall in love with you! Never! Not a chance in hell...I would rather die than have you within a 50-foot radius. You're pathetic and you absolutely disgust me!"

She closes her eyes and shakes her head; she suddenly hears a voice that seems to grow louder and louder. She thought that it was all in her head until Roman kept frantically looking around.

Unknown: Go away go away go away.... GO AWAY!!!

Suddenly the temperature dropped in the cabin. Roman could see his panicked breath immediately. Ice began to form on all the exposed wood beams. The mantra was repeating but only he seemed to be affected physically.

"Who is that? Where is it coming from?!"

The mantra was getting louder and louder causing Roman to fall to his knees covering his ears, screaming in anguish.

Kay could hear the voice as well, but it wasn't as loud as it was projected on Roman, she seemed to be in a safe and warm bubble from all the eerie happenings, but she had to admit, she was enjoying the show.

D: *Who is that? Kay, I've never heard this voice before!*

Kay: I-I-I don't know, Duchess, it just appeared! I wonder why we're not affected.

"Brady, did you hear that? The screaming, it's coming from that building. Let's go!"

Den and Brady head toward the dilapidated building shifting beforehand and creeping up towards it.

"MAKE IT STOP! Please..." Roman looked at Kay pleading for her help.

U: Don't you dare look to her for help, she can't help you...why would she? HMMM?! I won't stop until you tell the truth. You see, I can read your dirty, disgusting thoughts, Roman, so I suggest you confess your sins because your time is surely running out.

Roman is now shivering with the dropping temperature inside the tiny shack. He's stuck in the fetal position unable to move, hands clasped over his ears.

"Tell me what Roman? You didn't act alone...did you?"

He looks at her, but no words come out, his icy breath gasping for air that doesn't freeze his lungs creating a sharp burning pain.

"Answer me, dammit! Who put you up to this or I swear to the Moon Goddess..."

U: You better tell her, the amount of time you have of your pathetic miserable life is ticking by...

He's now shaking violently. "My father s-said if I h-h-help her I would get you as my prize. She wouldn't kill you if I kept you away. She wants to...to hurt your f-fam-mily. She used me to keep you away..."

"Away from who?"

"F-f-f-from y-y-our m-ma..."

The door explodes open and she can barely believe her eyes. His joy in his discovery is shown in the cloudy breaths forming as he steps forward. The tears constantly flowed down her face; she was unaffected by the severe cold.

"Brady? Please, get me out of here."

Brady noticed the lump on the floor and all the pain and rage of the ordeal came rushing forward.

"YOU!"

He grabs a crumpled frozen Roman and slams him against the wall and suddenly the room is warming back up.

Raven was in control, his claws out and all his teeth bared, and his usual black eyes burned red like a freshly stoked fire. He roars, shaking the structure, his Beta voice, though not as strong or powerful as an Alpha, was still quite intimidating.

"I ought to gut you where you stand! Give me one good reason I shouldn't flay you with my claws right now!"

Den takes the opportunity to free his sister. "Hurry Den, I need answers and he's going to kill him!"

He uses his claws to shred the rope and quickly hugs her before she brings her attention back to Brady and Roman.

"Brady, baby please! Raven, I know you want him dead but please...give Brady back control. We need answers...I need to know why...we need to know why. But I'm back, back in your arms. I need you to hold me, I missed you so much. Please..."

Raven looks at her hand on his forearm then looks into her eyes, eyes that held love, eyes that have been through a tough ordeal these past 24 hours and eyes that screamed to listen. Raven closes his eyes and inhales deeply a couple of times before he raises his eyelids again and there were the eyes that she indeed fell in love with.

"Baby girl?" She nods as his arms wrap around her and disposes of Roman in a heap on the floor, he pulls her away to check every inch of her.

His face fell when he didn't feel her or the sparks, she was right under him but couldn't sense her.

"He...he drugged you, didn't he?" He nearly broke out in tears, choking on his words.

She just nods her head. "With the same stuff from the party and a link blocker. I couldn't reach you; I couldn't sense you; I was so scared!" She squeezes him tighter. "But it's okay, it passed through my system quickly last time...we just have to wait. Will you wait...wait until the sparks come back. Please?"

He instantly nods his head, "I'd wait forever for you baby, you know that. I'm sorry I wasn't there to save you; I wasn't there to protect you. I'm so angry with myself for this, forgive me for not being there!" He falls to his knees and she embraces him against her body.

"This isn't your fault, if anything it's mine, I should have listened to you. You are not to blame, okay? I just want to go home."

Den clears his throat "Uncle Evan and Brent are on their way to take him to the dungeon."

She looks down and Roman meets her eyes, "She won't shut up! She keeps talking...torturing me. Make it stop! Make her stop, please!"

U: Ha! No, no dearest Roman not until you tell them everything and until then I am going to torture you subconsciously and I am going to enjoy every single second of it.

Roman starts to shake his head whispering "No" over and over as they take him away.

Back

O nce she was in view of the pack house her

mother ran towards her with her father not too far behind. They embraced so hard it looked like a collision filled with tears, sobs, and muttered apologies and finally smiles.

"I'm so happy you're okay, baby girl. I want you to go upstairs with Brady. It's been a long day, call down for room service and your mom and I will be in the guest bedroom for the rest of the week, we just want to be closer while we figure out all of this mess. Brady, thank you son for finding her, I meant what I said. I'm proud to call you son."

He pulls him into a hug. "Thank you, sir. That means a lot, it does."

Brady takes her hand and they go inside. Trini attacks her best friend, relieved to see her. "Kay, I'm so happy you're okay! If you want to talk later just buzz me." She nods as Brady follows her up the stairs.

"Kam, I hope you haven't completely pissed off the elders with you breaking the rules like that, baby doll." Kayd pulls Kam into him.

She glares at him. "Shut up! I did what I had to do to protect her! She was going to meet her soon enough, but she needed help now. I don't regret my interference one bit! She'll understand...she needed to meet her; she needed her help."

Brady hears the shower turn off and she steps out in a towel, another towel wrapped around her hair. She pauses at the door and gives him an innocent smile before going into the walk-in to grab her lounge clothes. She shakes out her hair as she tosses the towels in the hamper. She picks out her pink tank and boy short set and her thick cream knee high socks. She turns off the closet light and it's completely dark in their room minus the tv, she had blackout shades installed under her beautifully matched curtains.

She stretches before crawling into bed. Brady was in basketball shorts and pulled the blankets away from her side so she could climb in. She missed his touch but due to the drugs, couldn't feel the connection between them but she was glad to be in his arms again.

She slides in and sighs as she lays across his bare chest and he wraps his arms around her and squeezes, kissing her forehead.

Suddenly, she straddles him, and he sighs heavily.

"Baby...I'm already weak at your touch but this...is torture."

She leans down slowly placing her lips to his, pressing gently until emotion took over and it was a full blown make out session. She sits back up, panting with his hands still on her hips.

"Brady...", she whispered as her eyelids lowered. He sits up with her still in his lap. He brushed his lips along her neck and collarbone giving her goosebumps all over as she sighs.

There was lust in her eyes, in her touch, it seemed to radiate from her body. He watches her every movement keeping his emotions at bay because he doesn't want to take advantage of her. He missed her so much in that brief time, but he couldn't indulge in his temptations after what she had been through.

"Brady, I need you."

He shakes his head. "No, baby girl, you're not ready for that, not after what you've been through. As much as I want that, I can't take advantage of you, I won't."

She shakes her head and giggles, patting his chest. "No, I didn't mean sex. I want you to mark me. You're mine and I'm yours, right?"

"Absolutely, but are you sure? After all we've been through today?"

"It has been a rough day, but nothing made my heart beat more than when I saw you. Besides, I need to gain my Legacy powers, I was so helpless out there, I am one of the most powerful beings in the world and I couldn't even get away from a psycho junior high date. I need to protect myself, my family, you. But most importantly I want to get one step closer to being with you forever. I was daydreaming about our lives together when Roman left me alone. I imagined our wedding, I saw our children, I saw us so happy and it all starts with your mark. Please, my love..."

She pulls her strap down and away from her shoulder, looking back to give her approval as she tilts her head away. Her chest rises fast as she anticipates his lips on her skin. He lightly touches her shoulder grazing it down her arm giving her goosebumps, his lips follow the same path except upward, he punctuates each kiss.

"You have no idea how long I've been waiting to be with you, I love you so much Kayari Denise Miller."

Her heart drops and she freezes, her mouth wide open. "What did you just say?"

He laughs, brushing her cheek. "You heard me; I love you."

"No, no... I heard that exact phrase in my fantasies, my dreams. My mate was in my dream and he said...exactly what you said. It was you Brady, you were in my dreams."

Marked

Their eyes meet and in a silent approval he bares his teeth and sinks down into the crook of her neck. Like her mother, she doesn't make a sound above a wavering moan. Because she is an Alpha, she sinks her teeth deep and fast into the crook of his neck and he growls in pain.

"Oww! SON OF A... baby, did you have to be so..."

"Alpha like?" She smirks as she licks his wound. "Sorry, they said we have to be more aggressive in our marking. I'll make it up to you...I promise." He growls lustfully at her as she rocks back and forth.

She can feel the burning of her mark and she goes into the bathroom, there was the pack symbol and feeding below was her Legacy symbol. She smiled feeling content that she could tap into her white witch whom she named Tempest; she would start training in the morning.

As if reading her thoughts, she heard a voice.

U: No need for training, I have been in talks with Penelope and have learned everything she knows.

That voice...it was from the shack earlier no doubt about it.

Kay: Who are you?

U: Forgive my manners, greetings Alpha Kayari I am your white witch for which you have named me Tempest.

Kay: Tempest, was it you I heard in the cabin earlier? Threatening to torture Roman?

T: Oh, it's no threat. I plan on it.

Kay: How did you do that? I wasn't supposed to gain control over you until I was marked.

T: We lay dormant until then however under the circumstances of your kidnapping I was specially summoned. But we can talk about that later...your mate is calling you and standing at the door.

Kay looks over and sees Brady.

"Hey."

"Who were you talking to? I was afraid someone was in our room; my mother is still free, and I don't trust her."

"No, it was my witch, her name is Tempest. I asked her if she was the voice that was torturing Roman in the cabin and she said she was, but I asked her how because I don't get control until I'm marked but she said she was specially summoned. Do you know anything about that?"

"Not a clue but thank the Moon Goddess she was, is that why it was so cold when we came in, you almost froze him to death, not that I would be complaining."

She pulls him in front of the mirror. "Get under the light I want to see the mark on you."

He angles his neck and collar away so she can see the mark, she traces it with her fingertips causing him to shudder.

"Baby, that's my spot, you know that."

She pulls back. "Sorry, come on, let's get back to bed. I just want to watch movies for the rest of the day."

"Hey, can I ask you something that's been nagging me?"

"Sure." She pulls back the blankets.

"When you were at the refreshment table, why did you turn off your link? I tried to reach you to warn you, but you were completely shut off or...you blocked me?"

She sits on the bed pulling the pillow into her body. He sits beside her pulling a hand into his.

"Brady, you have to understand that before I found out about us, I was trying to understand my feelings for you. I thought I felt but then I didn't, I was struggling with what I wanted then Roman showed up and further confused me until he made me feel uncomfortable. I didn't want you to hear my thoughts when I had no answers myself. I'm sorry." She hangs her head, but he quickly lifts it by her chin.

"Hey, it's okay. You had every right besides, I was the one harboring the deep, dark secrets. I was the one who had the guilt eat me up every day. You shouldn't feel bad about needing time to think, I was curious but now I'm tired so can I finally, finally hold you in my arms?" He smiles as he attacks her neck and face causing her to giggle.

They lay in bed and he settles in the crook of her neck inhaling the weakest whiff of her scent. It still created butterflies and was a good sign because before he couldn't smell her at all. "Your scent is coming back, slowly but surely. It still drives me wild." She wiggles causing him to tighten his hold.

Two movies in and she had cabin fever. She convinced him to go downstairs to join everyone in the living room. Everyone was happy to see her smiling again.

"How is my Princess, did you--" Her mother cuts off her husband as she approaches her little girl, looking her over before her mouth opens wide. She just laughs as she holds her daughter. Figuring out her mom had put two and two together she simply nods, "It was only the mark, the other part will come later."

Hearing part of the conversation, Trini squeals and wakes the dead. "Oh. my. goodness, he marked you, didn't he? Didn't you?!" Den pulls her back onto the couch, telling her to be quiet and she instantly whispers a quick sorry.

"It's okay best friend and you're right he marked me as I marked him. I finally met Tempest and she said the oddest thing, mom you might be able to help me. She said that she was specially summoned to appear before I could gain control, do you know what that means?"

Kam looks at Kayd with a worried expression. "Honey, one day you will realize that you will do anything, and I mean anything for the lives of your children."

"Mooooom...what did you do? Was it you, did you somehow conjure up the power to get Tempest to help me?"

"I did what I had to do! I wasn't going to let someone take you from me and you were going to gain your powers soon...I just moved it along a bit. I would do it again if I knew you'd be okay."

"You could get in serious trouble for abusing your powers, mom. I can't be mad because you and Tempest saved me long enough before Den and Brady rescued me, but I'm still upset too, please mom you have to let me do this on my own." She sighs and hugs her mother. "Thank you, mommy."

Meet Alpha Damien

Brady pulls her to the loveseat besides Den and

Trini, the kids having their own conversation.

Kayd looks at Kam smugly, "Now how ironic that she tells you she can take care of herself, isn't that what YOU told ME? HMM?"

She stares at him straight-faced. "Shut up, if this is another one of your lectures then spare me, honey."

He pulls her into him and kisses her forehead. "No, baby doll, I only wanted to say thank you for saving our baby girl. You took the more sensible approach as I would have burned all the unclaimed land to the ground and tore that bastard in two. You are my better half, my rational girl." They share a kiss and then another until...

"Oh come on, mom, dad! Please, we're still here! UGH!" Kay gets up and goes to the kitchen.

T: Sorry to interrupt but have you thought about this whole plot-to-kill-you thing? I mean there is a fight coming and we need to know all the facts to put together a plan to stop this. I mean, your future mother-in-law is trying to kill you and we don't even know why.

Kay: I know Tempest and I am going to the dungeon tomorrow to talk to Roman and get my answers but in the meantime, I just want to enjoy my time with my family. By the way, she is not my mother-in-law, she means nothing to me..."

The slap echoed from the vastness of the throne room. Honestly, only selfish pricks owned a throne room to perch upon and look down at their peasants, a perfect description of Alpha Damien. "You said you could make the Miller family fall and I would be able to overthrow the pack! What a worthless whore you've become. Leaving your husband and son to seek revenge but your sister was just like you...chasing after a man... who *clearly* doesn't want you..." He looks down at her pathetically.

"SHUT UP!"

"You're as weak and pathetic as she was...you would have never been fit to be Queen; you don't even make a decent house servant so why do I still need you?" He grips her face tightly causing his long fingernails to puncture deep crescents into her face as she had done with her own son.

She panics breathing fast, unable to catch her breath. "We can still make it work, all I need to do is convince Brady to break her heart, he breaks her heart and she'll be too hurt to focus on the pack."

"Now why would he still listen to you? He made it crystal clear he has no qualms about killing you."

"I always have one trick up my sleeve..."

"Take this, it lasts for three days. It will cover the mark and your mate scent from them if you keep a considerable distance."

Kam hands him a vial.

"Yeah, I'd love to rid the world of this pitiful excuse of a woman and mother. I've made my peace with the fact that I will have to kill her, she means nothing to me."

Damn.

Even Kam was shocked by his icy cold statement. No one said anything.

He notices their reaction to his statement. "Sorry, I'm just ready to end this. Do you know she once told me that if I did have a mate that she would leave me because I was so pathetic and weak? Then when she found out about my Beta role, she said it would be temporary as she would make sure everyone felt the pain, she felt losing her sister. And when she did come into power, she would lock me up in the stockade so anyone could do whatever they want to me, what a mother to have, huh? She feels nothing towards me and is willing to let me be tortured. I feel nothing towards her except pure hatred."

Kam places her hand on his shoulder. "I'm sorry you had to endure any of this. You've always been a son to me, and I guess now it's official, you WILL be my son, but you've been nothing but a great friend to the twins, you were there for them and they were there for you. She knows nothing about you, and it shows. We know you and how wonderful you are, your dad and Gracie are so blessed to have you and so are we."

They share a warm hug, "Make her regret every single terrible thing she ever said towards you."

"No, stop! I BEG YOU! I'll tell you everything, just get out of my head!" Kay can hear Roman screaming, looks like Tempest had done what she promised, and broke him, maybe now she could get some answers.

Kay: Tempest, lay off, I can probably get everything I need now.

T: Awww, you're no fun! I was enjoying torturing this pathetic douchebag. He deserved it...you'll see...

With that, she cut off her link and you could hear Roman sighing in relief.

"She's only like that because she knows what you know, so tell me Roman...and don't lie because I can gladly bring her back. Now!" Her Alpha voice came in strong and commanding.

She leans against the cold bars awaiting his reply. He pulls himself together as he finally meets her eye. "I'm sorry, Kay but he's my father, I had to listen. Everything I said was true, I did fall in love with you instantly and I do love you, but I understand if you never do..."

"And you are right, Roman, I don't and never will. I have my mate. Now stop sugar coating and tell me first, who is your father?"

Although he was locked up in a dungeon, he was treated very humanely. He was fed, clothed, and kept clean; besides, it had only been one day. Contrary to popular belief, prisoners are not tortured incessantly...well...ok Tempest took it upon herself, that was different.

He sits on his bed, head hanging low and constantly rubbing his hands.

"My father is...Alpha Damien of the Rogue West pack."

"You mean the arrogant, power-hungry asshole who's shacking up with Brady's mother?"

He looks up, "Wait, *Carolyn* is Brady's mother?!"

I Can Make You Love Me

She nods and sighs, pinching the bridge of her nose,

"My mate and my ex-psycho prom date are this close to becoming brothers. Talk about a messed-up story."

"My father would never marry...that, she is beneath him and worth nothing more than a quick lay. He may be a rogue, but he has standards, he talks about her like she was a dish rag he found on the floor, good for a few uses but not clean enough to display on the countertop."

"Wow, harsh. But I don't care about her because she's trying to kill me. Why me, I was only a bystander in my mother's womb?"

"Because your mother is too powerful and causing your demise would work best in between commands and before you are marked." She nods and he continues, "Once you are marked you become stronger than your mother, right? So, the best bet is to get to you before then."

"Then why not go after Kamden? He doesn't have witch powers."

He shrugs, "I don't know that answer. She always swore she would destroy you and your mother."

She rubs her temples in frustration, "And you went along willingly?"

He looks up and then back down at his hands. "She said she was going to kill you, but my father said if I got rid of you instead that I could...you know, have you. That I could do whatever I wanted with you as long as I kept you away."

She could feel the bile again at the thought of what could have happened had he succeeded in his plan.

"I swear I was going to make you love me so that we could run away somewhere and live quietly raising our family, making love to you every night, sealing our love."

Well, that did it.

She violently heaved everything she consumed this morning onto the ground as she was gasping for air. The guards quickly called for someone to clean up the mess as she tried to push through the talk. They brought her a glass of water to wash out her mouth. After catching her breath, she felt the disgust build-up, Tempest had said she would see what a monster he was.

"You were willing to kidnap me, torture me, and eventually rape me just so you can live out your sick little fantasy?! Fair warning Roman, I *am* going to tell them every single disgusting detail you just told me and if my husband wants to castrate you and shove your balls down your throat, I would be ever so excited to watch. Tempest was right, you are a monster!"

T: Say the word, I'll turn him into a liquid right now!

"Is it rape if you want it? I would have made you want it, want me! I could make you love me if you just gave me the chance!"

"What. The. Fuck?! Do you hear yourself; you would have MADE me? You could make me; this is so fucking forced it's ridiculous! Let me break this down for you, Roman: I DO NOT WANT YOU OR ANYTHING TO DO WITH YOU! You make me physically sick and all I see is a rapist before me! I want nothing more than to be as far away from you as humanly possible and to be in the arms of the man who genuinely loves me and would never even consider forcing me to do anything. Don't you understand that you were contemplating torturing an Alpha? Do you know the consequences of even thinking like that?! You've already kidnapped me. You're going to die for your actions, Roman, hopefully, sooner rather than later. You better hope it is at the hands of my husband because Tempest wants to torture you thoroughly before she turns you into Jell-O! Literally, Jell-O!"

T: He doesn't realize he's in danger. I want to torture him for hours before I kill him in the absolute worst way possible. Sick bastard!

With those words, she walks out and back to the house. Her walk was slow and unsteady, she was lightheaded and dizzy, her hand clutching her queasy stomach as she linked Brady to meet her outside by the door. He doesn't hesitate and senses her duress, runs to her the rest of the way, and carries her bridal style to their room.

Once there, she chokes out what happened through the shaking and tears. She could see the rage forming in his eyes, Raven had made an appearance, his eyes black as night but not the fire red when his anger was out of control. "I should've killed that bastard the moment I saw him! I AM going to kill him the next time we cross paths, I'm going to castrate him and shove his balls down his throat!"

She bursts out laughing and all anger drains and Brady returns. He looked at her confused. "Baby girl, I don't see the humor." She motions for him to come lay beside her. "I know there isn't, but that was the exact same thing I told him you would do, word for word." He calms as he continues to inhale her scent which is growing stronger and stronger.

She purrs, "I have training with mom today to see what Tempest learned from Penelope and how to control my emotions. Did you guys come up with a plan?"

He sighs and backs away, she was not going to like it, but it had to be done.

A little while later, she shoots up. "Have you all lost your minds?! *That's* the plan? I'm not happy about this but if you think it'll work then...*sigh*, what choice do I have?"

They spend the next hour going over the details before she hops up to change into leggings, her blue sparkle sports bra and white crop sweatshirt. She heard a growl and before she could turn around, he had placed her on the counter in their walk-in. His hands were rubbing her thighs as he placed himself between her legs.

"Why does everything you wear have to be so sexy? How am I supposed to concentrate seeing you in that?" He leans in to tease her by licking her mark.

"Honey, you know we can't... I have training and you have to start the process."

He inhales her scent. "This blows, I won't be able to bask in your scent that drives me wild and I am growing tired of not feeling the sparks between us."

She gives him a big smile then a kiss on the lips, "Last time, we need to end this once and for all so I can spend the rest of my life with you." He reluctantly nods and presses his forehead to hers and they stay in silence for a few minutes, basking in each other. Finally, she hops down but he doesn't let her go, he wraps his arms around her and follows her down the stairs towards the open field where her mother was waiting.

"Brady, at some point you're going to have to let my daughter go so she can practice. Come on, I know what puppy love is, but she has to train, so do you." Kam watches as he whispers in her ear causing her to giggle and she turns around to wrap her arms around his neck as he leans down for one kiss that turns to two and then a few. They were so much like Kam and Kayd when they were younger it was completely adorable.

She clears her throat, "Okay you two we have a fight to prepare for. Brady, to the gym, and Kay you stand over here." With a final kiss, they separate to focus on their training.

Time to Train

*K*am: *Ok, now that you're marked your powers are strong and growing by the day. Now we must see what Penelope taught Tempest while she was dormant within you.*

Penelope: Everything I know. I learned several spells within the past few weeks that are the most powerful I have ever come across. Tempest knows them and knows the rules for their use. Also, she has a special power that I've never seen before. It's hard to describe but you'll see when push comes to shove.

Tempest: Penelope has been the best teacher and I cannot wait to unleash my full potential on those who wish to harm my family and my mate. I'll take them all on by myself!

Kam: Slow down there, Tempest. We are here to help with this. You don't have to do this alone. Just know that you are going to lead the charge. Okay, Kay/Tempest let's go over emotional control, the toughest aspect of all...

In the gym, Brady is running top speed on the treadmill with Den beside him. Den notices the aggressiveness in his run. His anger concentrated on the one sentence that broke his heart but also unleashed a wrath he had never felt before.

That bastard had planned to force himself on her, to take advantage, to defile her.

He was never going to ever get close enough to get that far ever again. To think that someone thought this was okay was sickening.

He maxed out on running completing ten miles and went to hit the weights. Den could hear his anger in his breaths while running but it was more obvious with the weights, he allowed them to slam recklessly with each rep. It fueled him, it allowed him to vent all his emotion before he had to switch his role.

"B, you okay?"

Den hands him his water bottle and he sits up on the bench shaking his head.

"No, I am far from okay. This plan has to work Den, I can't continue to look over my shoulder and have her living in fear. Do you know what she told me that Roman told her? He said that Alpha Damien told him that he could have Kay and take advantage of her as long as he kept her away. He was going to..." He chokes up every time he thinks about it. He squeezes his hands into tight fists to alleviate some of the frustration, it was either that or punch a hole into the nearest wall, concrete or not.

Den stops him. "Hey, it's not ever going to happen! Me, Dad, you, we would never allow anyone to harm her or any female in this pack."

Back on the field, Kay has practiced for the past two hours, sweat pouring from her body as she learned how to focus her emotions and the power of her spells towards a single point. She also learned that she could speak fluent Latin to cast the spells. She could feel the power coursing through her, she was stronger and more confident that she could defeat her, that's if she fought fair and she was smart enough to know that desperate people do desperate things. She wasn't going to play fair, not a chance in hell so she needed to be prepared for the unthinkable. Carolyn knew she could use Brady against her, and Kay would do anything to ensure he was safe.

All of this was exhausting, more so overwhelming, all she wanted was to find her true love and live happily ever after but just like in the movies there was always someone lurking who plans for your demise. She sighs as she wipes her face with a towel.

All of this got her to thinking about their mate bond and how it was incomplete. She was yearning for his touch already and honestly; it was all she could think about even after that disgusting conversation with Roman. She wanted Brady to romance her and sweep her off her feet before they shared their first time.

B: Hey you, go get dressed, we're going out tonight.

Kay: What...tonight? I just want to be with you...

*B: Kay, sweetheart, it will just be you and me, I promise.
I want to show you my commitment and love to you
before taking this potion to mask my mark and scent.
Come on baby, please.*

She couldn't resist him when his voice lowered an octave
trying to sweetly seduce her. And it was just what she
wanted before their first time, was he thinking the same
thing? She didn't know but she ran with it.

*Kay: Okay, I'm going to get ready now. Do not come in
while I am in the shower.*

He growls over the link.

*B: You're asking for a lot, baby girl. I suggest you beat
me there or I will join you.*

Taking You Out

She sprints to their room, stripping from the bedroom door to the bathroom door to rile him further. She melts as soon as the hot water hits her beautiful brown skin, she forgoes washing her hair as it would take forever to dry but she does spritz it with water to invigorate her curls. As she is applying light makeup, she hears him enter their room and the growl from seeing her clothes leading to the bathroom.

"You're quite the tease baby girl, you're going to regret that!"

She opens the door and steam rolls out to meet a lusty eyed Brady who looks like he is trying to will the towel off with his gaze. He bites his lip as she continues past and goes to their closet.

"Get in the shower!" She screams out because she knows he was about to follow her in. Defeated, he makes his way to the bathroom.

Kay looks at her choices and chooses that jaw-dropping gold dress from when she was picking out her party dress. She pairs it with strappy black platform sandals. She wears a black choker this time and a gold diamond bracelet her dad gave her for her 16th birthday. Finally, she adds her gold diamond hoops and looks in the mirror loving what she sees. She decides to bide her time so when the door opens, she knows he'll come into the closet to pick his clothes and see her in the mirror.

Sure enough, three minutes later the bathroom door opens, and he walks in with a towel wiping his face and hair until he catches sight of her and drops the towel in his hand. His mouth falls open and his hormones raging...

"Bloody hell...we're not going."

She smiles slyly as she shifts to look at him. "What? Why not I got all dressed up...for you." Her hands trail the curves of her body as she teases him.

"Baby girl..." He's clenching the towel wrapped around his body tightly as his eyes constantly wander over hers.

She turns and places her hand on his chest, feeling light tingles.

"Come on baby, this is your chance to romance me before we wage war. You promised..." She pouts, slightly whining to get her way.

He nods not wanting anything sexual to come rushing out of the thoughts he had...

"The gold dress though? You know how much I loved you in it at the mall and now I have to watch all eyes on you tonight?"

"Yes, but two very important things, you get to watch me walk from behind, and most importantly, I'm going home with you." She winks and saunters out, leaving him with that image. He sighs as he tries to calm himself down enough to get dressed.

He chooses a simple white button-down and blue trousers. He is buttoning his last button when their eyes meet. She is swooning at just how suave he is.

"Well, hello, handsome."

She walks over and pulls him down for a kiss.

"You look stunning, I meant to tell you earlier, but I was severely distracted."

She smiles innocently. "So where to?"

"It's a surprise, let's go."

They walk downstairs and into the living room where mom, dad, Trini, and Den were sitting. Den mind linked her earlier to help him because mom and dad were all kissy-kissy. She tells him to focus on the movie and turn the volume up.

Trini notices them. "Wow! Oh, I have got to get a picture of the pack's hottest IT couple, you guys look hot, especially my girl in that dress that I picked out!"

Her parents turn and their reactions are priceless. Mom gave her a thumbs up while dad was...well, dad.

"Kayari Denise...."

"Dad, don't start. Besides, I'll be with Brady." That statement seemed to short circuit his argument and he sighs in defeat.

Three hundred flashes later, "Ok, we have enough pictures, sheesh, this isn't prom. Let's go before it's too late." She waves at everyone before heading out the door.

He opens the door to his all-black Lexus, helping her into it as she loses a few inches in the dress she really didn't have as she sits down. She crosses her legs further accentuating them. She cleared her throat and he closed the door.

A thirty-minute drive into Lovingshire (Low-veng-shire) brought them to the new fancy Italian restaurant, Brigoni's. It was the newest addition to the small town but all the rage. The restaurant was two levels and Brady rented out the entire second floor.

He takes her hand as she adjusts her dress after gracefully stepping out of the car.

The valet bows, "Alpha, Beta, please make your way to the hostess who will seat you immediately."

They open the wood and glass adorned doors to a spacious family-style room. The hostess also bows her head before speaking, "Good evening Alpha Kayari and Beta Brady please follow me to your private table." The hostess smiles, blushing as she looks at Brady, and then he felt a squeeze as Kay was getting that look in her eye.

He squeezes back and she looks at him, "No need to worry gorgeous, I'm all yours."

Once seated it wasn't too long before a male waiter approached the table, bowing first.

"Welcome to Brigoni's, it is a pleasure to serve you Alpha Kayari, what can I get you to drink?"

Brady squeezed her hand then placed their joined hands on the table before letting out a low growl. He was proving his point without ripping his throat out. Brady was even more territorial of her after the kidnapping, so he made his point clear.

"Baby...he's our server and a member of our pack. Calm down please. Two waters for now, thank you."

He nods, walking away quickly.

"I know you want to protect me after what happened and I love you for it, just know that I'm yours and only yours. No one can take my heart from you."

She places a light kiss to his lips and he is at her mercy.

The waiter returns with their beverages. He takes their order, which Brady orders for them.

Brady opens his hands so she can place hers in his. Compared to his rough and strong hands that were hitting the weights earlier, her hands were soft and delicate.

They bask in a few moments of silence.

"We've been through a lot already and a lot more when we were friends and I wouldn't change it for the world. We are about to face something I never thought possible and though I've made peace with it, I'll still need your love and support afterward. As long as I have you my world is complete." He kisses her hands and she's trying to hold back the tears.

"That was beautiful. I am lucky to have someone willing to protect me and love me unconditionally despite all the obstacles in our way. You're amazing and I love you."

The air filled with emotion not only the love between them but from everything that has happened and the inevitable fight to save their pack. She wipes the tears from his eyes, and he does the same, causing her to laugh. "I didn't think dinner would be so emotional, haha."

He leans forward and kisses her.

"I love you."

"I love you, too."

"Would you do anything for me?"

"Of course I would, that should never be a question."

"Then marry me."

She giggles thinking he's teasing until she sees he's not laughing.

"You're serious?"

He pulls out a small red box, opening to a beautifully set three carat heart shaped diamond in a silver band surrounded in diamonds.

"It was all I could afford right now but I want to make this official, Kayari Miller will you marry me and become the future Mrs. Preston?"

She clutches her chest as the tears roll down her cheeks, unable to answer for a moment as she stares at his beautiful gesture of love.

He looks at her and smiles, "Are you ever going to give me an answer, baby girl?"

She hugs him, crying and whimpers out "Yes, I will." He places the ring on her finger, and she admires its beauty now on her hand.

"I love it, it's perfect."

He had been waiting two years to finally say, "I love you, Mrs. Preston."

Tonight was perfect.

Engaged

Lt is still early in the evening when they return, and

everyone is still on the couch.

"Have you guys literally been on the couch the whole time?" They all nod nonchalantly caught up in the action of the movie.

Trini glances up at them and screams like a banshee. "What is that?! Don't you hide it from me! OMG!" She hops up and is before them like a flash as she grabs her hand. She squeaks but nothing comes out except tears.

Shocking, Trinity McCallister couldn't utter a syllable.

She just pulls her best friend into a hug as her parents and brother try to gather what's happening. She tries to say something but once again is too in shock and she sits back down, waving Den away.

Kay puts her hand behind her back to ease the surprise on her approaching family. They all stand to look at the couple who seem to be hiding something.

"Dear Moon Goddess, you're not pregnant, are you?" Her dad looks at them, eyeing her abdomen.

"Wha-What? How dad? We're both virgins so no, quite sure I'm not pregnant."

He sighs heavily, leaning against the couch, "Well, that answers my second question. So, what's got Trini speechless? You know that's rare so it must be big."

Kay taps her index finger against her lips as if pondering, "Hmm, I wonder what it could be? Brady, do you have any idea?" He just shrugs as she leaves her hand in plain sight until...

"OH MY GOD, WHAT IS THAT?! Are you engaged?! You are! My baby girl, I'm so happy for you!" Kam takes over squealing duties for Trini who's still speechless.

Den hugs and kisses Kay on the cheek, "I'm happy for you, sis. You stood by your principles even after I ragged on you and now you are living the happiness you deserve. You've made me consider reevaluating my life, for real." He looks back at a still overwhelmed Trini then claps Brady on the back. "I guess we're bros officially now!" He sits next to Trini who is still crying and now squeaking. He holds her against him, rubbing her back.

She focuses back on her parents; her dad had his arm around his mother's waist, and she was holding his hand.

"Wow, it's like looking in a mirror. Remember everything we went through just to get where they are? It's so much worse now than then, I pray that we all get through this ordeal unscathed but...I just don't know this time. I don't want to put a damper on your engagement because I'm super happy for you, I'm just...being a mom and worried. My beautiful girl and now my handsome son, I just want this done and over so I can see you walk down the aisle." She sniffles as she hugs her and then heads to their guest room.

"She'll be fine, I promise, it's just a lot to take in especially with your family coming back for revenge. It's just an obstacle but shouldn't get in the way of your happiness. I love you baby girl and you too, son." He smiles fondly as he follows his wife into their room.

Brady wraps his arms around her and kisses her gently, "Well, my beautiful fiancée let's go to bed. We've had quite the eventful night."

She sighs, "And it only gets worse tomorrow, at least I'll be in your arms tonight."

"And for the rest of our lives."

Finally, after calming down, Trini catches their attention. "Love you guys!" Kay smiles and nods, "Thank you, my maid of honor. Goodnight." Trini looks shocked and again is speechless.

Kay stops at the door and looks over her shoulder, glancing at him then down in the direction of the zipper of her dress. "Babe, could you?" He was standing behind her and in a perfect position to help, she was also teasing him.

He gazes at her gorgeously sculpted back before placing his hand on the zipper, sliding it down slowly as it opens. Halfway down she opens the door and takes the zipper from him, glancing upward. "Thanks, doll." She steps in and walks into the bathroom. He hadn't realized he was following her like a lost puppy, eyes still roaming her back and her backside and most importantly her legs which he wanted wrapped around his...

"Baby!"

He snaps to attention when he realizes he is in the bathroom with her.

"It's like you were in a trance, are you okay? I know you want to keep me safe, but I can shower on my own." She gives him a quick peck.

"Oh I know, I was mesmerized by you and my mind wandered elsewhere. Here, let me run a bath, you need to relax those muscles you've been working so hard. Go grab your sleep clothes and I'll get it going.

She smiles slyly, she had to admit her thoughts were all over the place now that he had professed his love. She went into the closet and chose another short and cami set, this time all black, she also grabs his black silk pajama bottoms for him to change into.

She walks back to see him pouring lavender oil and adding a bath bomb to the water, the aroma was amazing. He dims the overhead lights and lights a few candles. She comes in and finds her radio station to play in the background. She places her clothes down and places his pants beside her and he raises an eyebrow.

"I want you to lay with me, our date isn't over yet, let's end it on a high note. I want the memories while we play into their little game. No matter what happens, you're mine and I'm yours, okay?" He nods, their plan begins tomorrow, and although the toughest thing they'd have to do they knew in the end that they would be coming back to each other.

She slides out of her dress and he holds his hand out to let her slip into the warm water as she sighs in content. He hops in, but still in his boxers, and she looks back at him in question.

"Listen, baby, I have zero willpower at the moment, the fact that you're naked in front of me right now is a big hurdle. This keeps me within the boundaries I set because I want to wait until after this is over to spend the night making love to you."

"Yeah, but you've seen all of me and now I am curious..." She giggles but leans back against him.

"Well, you didn't have to get completely naked."

"Babe, you said a bath which means naked or else we could have just gone down to the Jacuzzi but no worries." She sighs as she sinks lower to cover herself in water and bubbles. She can feel his heart beating faster and she just laughs.

"You okay?"

He nods and wraps his arm across her shoulders.

"Perfectly fine, sharing a relaxing bath with my wife and eventually the mother of my children."

"Just how many are we talking about?"

He kisses her temple, "As many as you want to give me. One, six, a dozen...doesn't matter."

Her eyes bug out at the last number and she scoffs, "I'll tell you that the last one isn't happening, not on your life buddy! We only have three weeks before the next full moon too and mom says my heat will be like giving birth but four times as painful due to being a wolf and a Legacy. Luckily, dad set up a romantic weekend and they "fixed" the problem, ironically that's when we were conceived."

He wraps his fingers with hers, "Well, then that's what will happen, I will whisk you away somewhere."

After a few moments, he notices she has gone quiet and looks down to see her eyes closed. She was a stunning beauty even when she was asleep.

He kisses her temple, whispering "We are going to win this, I can do this as long as I know I have you." He shakes her slightly, "Sweetie, it's time to get out." She moans as she wraps her arms around him facing him. It felt magical to be in this position, but it was time for them to get some sleep. He pulls the tub stopper, lifting her but standing her up. Her eyes were glazed over, but she was able to stand on her own as he wrapped the towel around to dry her.

He slips on her cami and shorts and leads her to bed and she happily accepts the warmth of her blankets while he runs back and slips out of his boxers and into his pajama bottoms. He puts their towels away in the hamper and turns out all the lights. He opens the curtains of one of the floor-to-ceiling windows to let the moonlight in as it casts a twilight across her body.

She's talking in her sleep and he slides in just as she sighs, "Mmm, Brady, please...I need you..."

Those words cause his blood to rush south as he bites his lip. "She's going to be the death of me..." He pulls her into his chest and kisses her forehead.

"Mmm...night, baby."

He smiles looking down at her and her beautifully adorned ring finger. "Goodnight, baby girl."

The Plan

It was the morning of the plan and Kay was up at 7 am on the balcony watching the world exist. The world seemed quiet and more peaceful than what she was about to come across, so she basked in it.

The groundskeepers were attending to their manicured lawn and bushes, it was time to plant the spring flower selection her mom had picked.

She ran through her part over and over. The plan was more complex now that she knew the pack had a mole feeding information to Alpha Damien and Carolyn, for what gain, she had a suspicion.

Kay pulls her robe together as she walks back inside to a still slumbering fiancé. She walked over to her jewelry box and sighed loudly. He had done such a wonderful job in picking out her engagement ring that it pained her to take it off, but it was temporary. For the fight of their lives. She relishes in its perfectly designed beauty. She wouldn't have known what to pick, the choices were overwhelming.

For a moment she wallows in sadness as she couldn't help but allow the bad thoughts to raid her mind, what if this didn't work? What if they lose reigning pack status? What if...

She's jolted back into reality by soft lips on her shoulder and arms around her waist.

"Good morning, beautiful. Stop thinking like that, we need to keep thinking of our outcome our way or it won't work."

She's stunned, "How did you know?"

He pulls her chin up to see herself in the mirror. "Because you crinkle your nose when you're upset." He rubs the wrinkled area and his touch calms her and she chuckles.

He turns her to face him. "We can do this, okay?"

His forehead touching hers. "I really don't like her. I'm going to enjoy ripping her apart."

He was surprised by her viciousness. "Baby, she's irrelevant and you'll need to keep your cool if the plan is to work. You know this will all be an act; we need to expose all involved and then..." Tempest cuts him off.

T: REVENGE! Sweet, glorious revenge to those trying to take my mate and my pack from me.

She chuckles, "Well, Tempest is more than ready. One word for her: revenge. I mirror her sentiment."

She changes gears as she wraps her arms around his neck and pulls him in for an intense make-out session. He squeezes her hips a little tighter than normal trying to get as close as possible. When they finally break apart, she lets a moan slip out causing her to bite her lip. He growls and smacks her bottom before heading towards the bathroom.

"I'll run a bath, okay? I promise to get naked this time." She nods, blushing immensely. She goes into their closet choosing their clothes.

Damien's mole was here today, they had slept over last night but weren't in the vicinity when they came back engaged so they would work that angle. Kay could smell that gaudy cheap perfume a mile away no matter what part of the house they were in and this morning, sure enough, the rank smell was in the air.

It wasn't clear until a few days ago that someone was funneling information to Alpha Damien, but the reason why was still a mystery. Once they realized who it was, they decided to use it as an advantage, and they would be none the wiser.

Their bath was relaxing as he washed her and whispered sweet nothings in her ear, and they finished up with a prayer to the Moon Goddess for the protection of their pack and especially their love.

Once dressed they linked Trini and Den and told them the show was about to start. They agreed and were in the kitchen with the mole already.

She takes the deepest breath of her life. "Ready? Remember I don't mean the harsh things I'm going to say." She kisses him.

"Me either, I love you, Mrs. Preston."

She smiles at her new moniker before letting her face fall as she opens the door.

"**O**H, FUCK YOU, BRADY MARSHALL

PRESTON! You didn't think I would find out you slept with Yaya?! We're supposed to be together, we're supposed to be an example, and you go whore it up with her? You fucking disgust me…ugh!!!"

She stomps down the stairs with him following her into the kitchen. When she sees her brother in his place she whips around with her finger in Brady's face.

"I should have known you would do something like this, hanging out with HIM. YOU'RE A MANWHORE JUST LIKE HIM!"

He reaches for her hands, but she yanks them back roughly. She uses that momentum to her advantage and slaps him harshly across the face. The whole room went deathly silent.

"DON'T you ever touch me again! You are nothing to me…*beneath* me and I shouldn't even have let myself think you were EVER worthy of me. So, this, whatever this shady ass bullshit was, is over. We are over! I regret every single day we ever spent together. Enjoy your many diseases...I'm sure you've already racked up." She shoots daggers as Den stands beside her.

"Why are you two in a screaming match and what is going on?" Den growls at his best friend.

She turns to her brother, "Didn't you hear, your best friend decided he'd rather shove his dick in any and everything than wait for the girl who loves him."

Brady shrugs nonchalantly, "Well if she wasn't so damn high and mighty, I could have satisfied my needs with her, but the princess here wouldn't allow it, so I let Yaya do it for me and I don't regret a single stroke or moan of my name from her lips one bit. In fact, I may go back for round FOUR...I enjoyed having her writhe under me screaming my name climax after climax. She could really take it!"

Kay lets out a vicious roar with Den struggling to hold her back.

"Your morals are as ass-backward as you are! You just want someone for sex, by all means go ahead but I won't lower myself to you. Sleep with whoever you want, as of this moment you are no longer our Beta and we are no longer together. Now get out before I rip your worthless dick off and feed it to the dogs. Oh never mind, I would never feed such beautiful creatures... scraps." She viciously eyes him up and down.

Brady was red in anger but none more than the handprint across his face. He was also pleasantly shocked at her words. She said she would wing it for it to feel more natural. She was good, he had to give her that.

He steps forward but Den instantly steps in front of her, fists clenched. "She's my sister man, you better choose wisely, I would end you over her any day. Especially after what I'm hearing." Den and Trini bare their teeth all the while the mole watches on...her mouth turned up into a smirk. She was enjoying the show.

Brady steps back and looks at all of them. "Whatever, this pack will fail without me and as for our friendship, our brotherhood...I guess you'll always pick a bitch over me, huh?"

He saw the shock briefly in Den's eyes and the hurt in hers. He had to stay in character no matter how much it hurt. It was all about winning the war, not the battle.

"Why don't you take your worthless ass out of my face, my house, my life! I wish you were my mate so I could reject you so you can feel the pain I do!"

The tears flow out easily but as much as he wanted to console her, he backs away instead.

"I would never want someone like you as my mate. A cold, emotionless, prudish, spoiled fucking princess who will most likely be terrible in bed and I don't have the time to teach you. There are plenty of girls willing to satisfy me and know exactly what to do to get me off."

He looks over at the mole and winks.

Oh, her blood pressure shot up instantly. Her anger was borderline real now.

"Brady Preston you are by far the sorriest person I have ever met, you were never worthy of an Alpha female, at best these bitches who screw you for power, that's all they want you for anyway, but now you don't even have that. I banish you from the Cheshire pack effective immediately! I wish you nothing but the worst."

His chest heaves up and down in rage and anger, once again stepping forward but Den gives a warning growl.

"You heard her! Get the fuck out Preston!"

He turns around walking away then stops, "Oh, my mother was right about you, all of you. I would be more than happy to help her cause your demise. This is far from over!" He storms out slamming the door loud enough to rattle the house.

Her brother's arms wrap around her and Trini hugs her other side. Through their arms she can see the mole sneak out to follow Brady, the door barely squeaks open and closed.

"She fell for it. Link him to let him know."

"Already done so he can work phase two." He wipes his sister's eyes and smiles. "You did good, I thought you were going to kill him where he stood."

"Oh, he's not the target of my rage, but she is. She better enjoy the time she has left..."

Brady pulls his keys from his pocket, fumbling angrily. He slams his fists on the roof and groans loudly. "Fucking bitch!"

"I told you I was the better choice, but you ran after her. I know what you want, what you need. I could still make that happen..." Her finger traces his chest when he faces her.

"Get in the car." She smiles and saunters over to the other side. Her already short shorts were riding further but that's exactly what she wanted, to tease and seduce. She squeals, placing her hand on his upper thigh, inching closer and closer while licking her lips.

"Not right now but soon. I'll have you screaming my name in no time. But first...I need to speak with my mother."

She nods and enjoys the ride to Alpha Damien's house.

You Were Right, Mom

His mother walks out when she hears him peel into the driveway, slamming his door mumbling the entire time. He stands before her but far enough away she doesn't sense his mark or scent.

He throws his hands up and falls to his knees, "You were right, is that what you wanted to hear, to see your son broken by that Miller bitch and her family? Well, congratulations mother, I look like a class A fool and now I'm crawling back."

She seemed skeptical, "Why didn't you go back to your father?"

He laughs hysterically, "You mean the former Alpha's lapdog, are you kidding me?! He would just tell me how wrong I was and that I should apologize, which I will NEVER do, you hear me?! I would rather die first."

He pants while she looks him over, assessing the situation before her.

"Can you confirm everything he says?"

Melody looks up. "Oh yes, I was there to witness it all, they are on extremely bad terms and he even swore revenge on them in your name. You should have no problem extracting information needed to rid us of that wretched family."

His head was down but a look of shock on his face as she spoke so calmly like she had won him as a prize. Well, he had to play the game to win, so he stands up and slides his arm around her waist. She was so delighted by his claim, she may have been close enough to detect the mark and scent, but she was too stupid in love to notice.

His mother smirks, "Looks like you've already found your rebound, son. I'm sure you know now that we placed our little Melody into the pack to find the information we needed to take them down but looks like she also got what she wanted, which was you."

He leans down and kisses her forehead, his stomach an ocean of waves. He had to take in a few deep breaths while trying not to empty his stomach. Everything about her was wrong, her touch, her smell, that stupid smile on her face but he had to power through.

"She's not a rebound, she's who I should have picked in the first place, I hope she can forgive my stupid mistake, guess I was power-hungry." She just nods.

"Well, shall we retire into the house so you can give us the information we need? Alpha Damien will be so pleased!"

He sighs, "Absolutely, but can I have some time alone to just wrap my mind around what happened? It's exhausting."

"Sure son, I'll let Alpha Damien know what happened and Melody will confirm what she saw. You get some rest, recharge your battery." She and Melody make their way to Alpha Damien's office with the wonderful news.

Brady finds an empty guest room and flops onto the bed. "UGH, I need to bathe in acid, but a hot shower will do. I hope my princess is faring better than me..." He walks into the in-suite bathroom to wash the grime, known as Melody, off his body.

Meanwhile, Kay walks down to the dungeon with more tears running down her face as she chokes back sobs just as Roman lays his eyes on her. He is concerned, not worried about her outburst from the other day.

"Kayari, what's wrong?" He walks up to the bars that separate them.

"Well, you were right, I hope you're happy! My life is completely ruined, maybe even my reputation! How will other Alphas trust me if I can't even sense that my mate was a lying, conniving, manipulative bastard! That's right, he cheated on me and why? Because of my morals and values that I wouldn't give it up to him just yet, what a fucking waste of a werewolf. Now I have no mate, no Beta and I look like a fool. I made the whole pack look weak!" She lets the tears gather before looking at him glassy-eyed.

"Why did you have to be right, Roman, all I wanted was my happiness, my true love. I wanted him to love me as much as I thought I loved him. I..." She couldn't continue.

Roman places his hand on hers. "I love you Kayari, I will always love you. I should have just waited for that bastard to show you his true colors and I would have swept in to save you from his lies. I-I'm still here for you if you'll have me. I would never cheat on you; you're the perfect woman and he is a damn fool to not see that."

She is swallowing the bile rising in her throat and she chokes it down. "Thank you but I just need some time. I can't believe I was so stupid! Can we change the subject, are they treating you okay here?" She wanted to give him a shred of care when she knew he was going to rot in here.

"Yeah, I guess. I will say the food is amazing. I hate to push it, but will you visit me tomorrow? Your company keeps me going." He rubs his thumb across her hand, and she forces a small smile. "Sure. I'm emotionally exhausted. I'll talk to you tomorrow."

Though the performance was draining she was going to the gym to practice her spells she would need for the inevitable fight.

Around 11 pm, Brady calls from a burner cell. They needed no traces of their communications during their "fight".

"Hello?"

"Baby, I miss you so much, your smile, your eyes, your touch. I miss lying next to you at night. I can't wait for this to be over so I can make you mine finally. Say something sexy for me so I can dream about you tonight."

"I might, baby, depends on who's in bed with you? Where is she?"

She, of course, was referring to Melody.

"I convinced her to let me sleep alone tonight due to my broken heart about a certain ex-girlfriend. I must admit I had to kiss her on her forehead, it felt so gross. I took the hottest shower in my life to get her off me."

She growls then laughs, "She's going to move fast now that she thinks you're so heartbroken. Keep the touch to a minimum or you will have a problem with me, got it?"

"Of course, my baby girl. Jealousy sounds very sexy on you. What about you, are you okay?"

"Yeah, I went to Roman, and as predicted he was more than willing to start picking up the pieces to my broken heart. He rubbed on my hand and I almost lost my lunch."

Brady growls low and long.

"Brady, sweetie, it's just part of the plan."

"So is me tearing him in half..."

"Ooh, you sound so sexy when you're mad, mmm..." She starts to purr, his weakness.

"Dammit baby, you're such a tease. Now I have to take care of this myself."

She sighs, "Sorry, baby. It won't be too much longer, I promise. And as for saying something sexy for you how about, I can't wait to feel your strong hands over my warm body that's blazing just for you, I want you to kiss every inch of me, have your name on my lips and then and only then do I want you to make love to me."

The line was silent for a while before he exhaled. "Oh baby, I have to get off this phone before this becomes a whole session, but I will grant your wish when I get back, I love you, Mrs. Preston, you are my world."

"And I love you, Mr. Preston, you're mine and I am yours."

With that, they hang up and he hides his phone, tomorrow was another day.

"Carolyn, you can't be that stupid, can you?"

"He's my son! And Melody saw it all, how much more convincing do you need? Yes, he was angry with me for leaving him when he was a child, but he'll always want my love and now we can use that to strengthen our plan. He's completely torn down and if we can build him up, offer him a role as your Delta or Omega, he will bend to your will. He'll be the ultimate weapon against them!"

Alpha Damien looks down at a kneeling Carolyn, he wasn't as quick to trust him though if true, he would be a tremendous asset. He taps his glass of scotch with his nails allowing himself to bask in her groveling.

Melody was standing beside her, her head bowed.

Too bad she was obsessed with that boy, he thought. She'd be perfect as one of his concubines, she has a young, filled out body with ample breasts and plump pink lips. She was the newer model of Carolyn who he was growing tired of but had to keep her around, after, it didn't matter. Perhaps if he killed her and Brady, he could have Melody. He smirked thinking of having that nubile young she-wolf under his grasp while Carolyn awaited an answer.

"Very well but what good is he if I already know what he knows?"

"That's where you are wrong, Damien, you don't know everything. I knew you wouldn't trust me outright; I'd be crazy to assume you would, but I have a juicy tidbit that will prove my loyalty to you."

Brady walks down the long aisle up to where Carolyn looked as if she was begging.

Typical

Melody stood next to her, who was beaming at the sight of him. He had to avoid being too close again, so he stood on the opposite side of his mother.

"It's *Alpha* Damien to you, boy. Now, what is it that I don't know?"

Brady scoffs, he was no Alpha, he gave himself that title in a power-hungry move. He had followers but they were no real pack, he had no Beta, Delta, or Omega. He was a tyrannical monster who ran whatever this was his way. He had no power to challenge any real pack but here he was trying to overthrow the most powerful one. Arrogance will get you killed every time but that's what Brady wanted, he wanted every person in this room to die a miserable death and he was getting closer to his goal.

He tilts his head and smiles devilishly. "Mother, get up, this man holds nothing over you, and you deserve not to be disrespected."

He holds his hand out and he stands far enough away to help but still mask everything. She smiles at the first kind gesture from her son.

She now stands watching the exchange between her lover and her son. She knew Alpha Damien wasn't good for her and he treated her like a servant, but she was desperate to exact revenge for her sister. She even thought when they won, she'd stab him in the back and watch his blood spill and she would take all that was his. He had no mate anymore and had been a rogue his whole life, she would keep the castle for herself and all his possessions. Oh, the power she'll feel sitting on his precious throne!

Brady walks up and stops just before the steps that lead to the throne.

"You say your plan is in order? You got everything covered and you're waiting for the perfect moment to pounce? Tell me, *Damien*...where is your son? Wasn't he part of the plan? When was the last time you spoke to him? I can answer that for you, it's been three days, almost four, hasn't it?"

He smirks knowing he was right while Carolyn gasps at the revelation.

He could see the anger boil within him. He stands and rushes Brady slamming him against the nearest wall he could find. "WHERE. IS. MY. SON?!?!"

Damien was a filthy rogue and he didn't believe in the mate bond so he wouldn't be able to smell it. Being so close was not a problem, anyway, he was too enraged that Brady knew they had his son.

Brady laughs in his face, angering him further. He touches his lip and notices the blood, the force of the impact causing him to bite his tongue.

"What a great father you are! You would have gone another few days without even thinking of him but he's part of your plan, right? You are a pathetic Alpha, but you are an even worse father!"

That earned another slam against the wall and a vicious growl while he bared his teeth. "For someone who has nothing and lost everything you are not in the situation to gain any more enemies, so I suggest you tell me where my son is now." He was calm, too calm.

Brady easily removes his tightly clenched hand from his collar, pushing him far away. "Yeah, and they have your son locked away in their dungeon doing who knows what. Maybe he's so weak he's spilling your plan to them; wouldn't that be karmic?! He's a liability and you didn't even know it! How comical! So, there's your tidbit of information, do I have your attention now?"

Vital Information

Kay awoke a little later than usual this morning, she lay in bed trying to continue her dream world with her fiancé but to no avail. She also knew she'd have to visit Roman again and was trying to stomach it. She drags herself into the shower, blasting the coldest water to wake her up.

She reaches the kitchen to see Den and Trini snuggled up and at that moment she really missed her fiancé. She makes her way to the fridge to grab the orange juice.

Sensing her frustration, they separate into their own personal spaces.

"Don't mind me guys, I'm okay I promise, I just hate this." Trini wraps her up in a hug.

"Don't worry in no time I'll be harassing you about bridesmaids' dresses, wedding colors, cake flavors, and if you want to go to Tahiti or the Maldives for your honeymoon, this fight is big but the reward so much bigger!" She nods and sighs, trying to motivate herself to continue.

After a light breakfast, she changes and goes down to the dungeon with his meal, a small gesture that says they're okay.

"Roman? Are you awake?" He was lying there, arms behind his head, legs crossed but couldn't contain his smile as he saw her with his food. She places it on the tray that opens to his side to where he can grab it. He sets it down right beside the bars and sits down. She joins him on the ground watching him eat.

"How did you sleep?" He shrugs before gazing at her.

"You look really beautiful today; I mean you do every day but especially today. Sorry, I'm rambling..." He looks down at his tray.

She gives him a comforting smile. "Thank you, that's really nice of you especially in the situation you're in."

He slides the tray to the side and faces her, the bars covering up her beauty with their harsh cold lines. "Thank you for breakfast and I promise you I will make all this up to you..."

"Roman..."

"No, Kay, you deserve to be happy and I want to be that for you."

"I still need so much time Roman, not only because of the Brady fiasco but also what you said to me, I just can't trust anyone right now with my heart. Can you understand that?" He nods, not trying to push her buttons too much.

"So, tell me, how did you end up in California with your mom? Why did she leave your dad?"

"Are you pumping me for information?"

She laughs loudly, "Haha, for what? You're already in our captivity. No, I was simply curious how our story ended the night you left for California. I mean, you don't have to tell me. I-I'm sorry, I'll leave if you want..." She turns to get up, but he places his hand on hers.

"No, don't go! I want to tell you what happened besides, I like spending time with you even in these circumstances." Again, she flashes a curt smile.

"My mom fled with me after the dance, but I begged her to let me stay and live out my one dream which was to take you to this dance, but I had to agree to leave right after. There was nothing I could do, I had to leave with her. My dad was abusive and violent, and she couldn't take it anymore. The sad part was that he didn't even look for us, he didn't feel the pain of the strain on their mate bond, or he simply didn't care. One night, my mom fell to the floor and was in excruciating pain as it was clear, he had slept with someone else. She endured it the first time but she found a witch doctor that cast a spell so she could no longer feel the betrayal and broke their mate bond."

She felt sad for his mother, she couldn't imagine feeling that pain from your mate sleeping with someone else, she was glad she found a way to avoid any future pain.

"I vowed I would come back and seek revenge on that miserable bastard! NO ONE hurts my mother; I don't care who they are! I want to spill his blood on this Earth and to do that I had to come crawling back under the assumption that I had grown a hatred towards my mother. I wanted him to think that I wanted to gain power under him to possibly take over."

She stares in awe of all this added info, where she once wanted to rip out his vocal cords with her teeth, she now realized she could use Roman, now she had to determine if she trusted him enough to reveal her big plan. She would discuss it with everyone first.

"How long have you been back?"

"Only a few weeks, enough time for him to beam about his son coming back and wanting to rule all the land before him. Then I met Carolyn, what a piece of work! I thought my dad was crazy, but she is on another level! Her plot for revenge was all she could talk about; I honestly think my dad slept with her to shut her up. Apparently, he'll sleep with anything. Anyway, one day she approached me with my part of her plan and my dad counteroffered your murder with me absconding with you somewhere to live life happily ever after." She holds up her hand, her other clutching her stomach, the nausea returning with a vengeance. "Please, I can't handle that right now."

He nods, "I'm sorry and I am willing to spend the rest of my life apologizing. I could never push you to do something against your will, I don't know why I thought I could. Guess the apple didn't fall too far from the tree, huh? It was a disgusting thing to think about." She could only nod in agreement.

She spends another 30 minutes talking and discussing before she stands up saying she had to go to practice. He once again asks her to visit and she agrees. After all the information she got from today, she was going to squeeze him for everything he knew!

She relays everything to her brother and best friend who look at her like she has gone mad.

"Nope, no way in hell! And sis, you're crazy if you believe him. He planned to kidnap and rape you and now I'm supposed to work WITH him when I'd rather rip him apart?" He shakes his head and waits for Trini's response. "I don't know, it's too early to make a decision. If we can use what he knows for us, then good but we also have to keep our guard up."

Den laughs aloud, "Remember your soon to be husband? Yeah, he will not go for this, at all! He is going to lose his shit, but by all means, tell him." He walks away confident because he was right, Brady was his best friend and he knew him better than anyone. How would she convince him?

Around 11 pm again, she calls him this time.

"Baby girl?"

"Hiiii, baby I miss you soooo much, so so so much. Have I told you how much I love you, today?"

There was a pause. "You sound too sweet even with us being apart, what's going on?"

She drops the act and takes a deep breath and tells him everything to which he replies, "Not a snowball's chance in hell! I don't even like this part of you being near him without me but to trust that bastard, hell no. When this is over, I am going to enjoy ending his life!"

She tries to calm him down. "Listen, I will keep my guard up, but he is providing some useful information. I agree to not tell him our plan, but we shouldn't count him out just yet. Trust me, baby, please."

All she heard was growling so she counters by purring and using her sexiest voice.

"Please? I promise to be careful. As your wife, I'm asking you to let me try."

"Riri, baby, don't do that, you know what it does to me."

She continues, "Mmm, but I miss you so much. I had the wildest dream about us last night. Hot doesn't even begin to describe all the naughty things you did to me."

She paused because she could hear him panting. "Grrr...you're not playing fair, baby girl, using my situation against me. Alright, but I want you to be careful he may be double-crossing you; I still do not trust him one bit. Now... tell me your fantasy about us..."

She smiles devilishly as she goes into full unadulterated detail.

The next morning Brady gets a knock on his door. Still sleepy he stumbles to the door and opens it without regard.

Melody purrs as she eyes his package. "Mmm, nice. Hey baby, I'm making breakfast if you're hungry." He quickly shifts behind the door and puts on his best heartbroken act.

"Melody, I'm still hurting pretty badly so I'd be okay if you're not ready to wait for me, I already hurt you enough by you watching me with her every day. You didn't deserve that." He lets his head fall to complete the pathetic look, but she takes his hand.

"I've been waiting for you to come to your senses and not follow behind her like a lost puppy, as long as I'm the only one, I can wait." She smiles looking at their joined hands.

His shower would be nuclear today, he wondered if he could function with only one hand as he really wanted to gnaw his off right now.

She breaks his trance, "Come down for breakfast...after you take care of that...or... I could help." She licks her lips, eyeing her prize. He hides behind the door more; it was the typical morning situation coupled with what Kay told him last night.

"Thanks, honey but I desperately need a shower. I'll be down in twenty." She smiles and heads to the kitchen.

He shudders to think of all the places she touched him and her eyeing his package, his appetite long gone.

He goes to scrub off several layers of skin from his body.

"NO! Stop, please! Don't hurt him! Please...no!

"Kay! Wake up!" She sits up panting and shaking, cradled by arms that were not his but her brother's.

"Kamden?" He hugs her, "You were screaming bloody murder, I didn't know if you were okay! I almost called the warriors from their practice to dispose of whoever it was harming you."

She finally stops shaking and pulls her hair into a high ponytail. She's still breathing heavily trying to explain what happened in her dream.

"Wow, it all seemed so real! I almost thought I lost you and Brady, we were surrounded, and Brady was trying to save me, and someone came from behind and... and... oh Den it was awful! I can't lose you or Brady, you guys are my backbone. I know we fight a lot, but I love you so much." She hugs him tightly.

"Kay, I can't breathe! I'm not going anywhere, see? Right here."

His statement calmed her a bit. He smiles and holds her hands in his.

"What are we doing, Den? We're barely into our reign and chaos has already ensued. Our pack must think we're insane. I can only imagine the rumors especially since they don't know the actual plan. They probably think I'm some hot-headed, temperamental, cold-hearted, frigid bitch."

"They thought that before our reign, no I'm just kidding. They must understand that we are at war; they don't need full detail, just to fight for your pack. Their loyalty is to our family, our pack. Speaking of plans, you plan on visiting *him*?"

She laughs hard. "Really, *him*? Don't be petty, Den Den."

He growls, "You know I hate that!" He pushes her into her pillows.

"Duh! That's why I said it to get on your nerves as a sister is supposed to do." She pauses then her smile is a mile wide, "Soooo, not to change the subject but I see that you and Trini have been mighty close lately. Could it be? Could my brother be in l..."

He covers her mouth quickly. "Don't you dare. Okay, you were right, I really do like her, she's sweet and kind and doesn't look at me for my role as Alpha. She truly is the perfect girl."

Her mouth falls open, but no words come out, just a squeak.

He raises an eyebrow at the noise, hardly able to hold his laughter. "What in the world was that?"

She covers her mouth with her hands and then drops them. "I'm just so happy for both of you, I know we have different values when it comes to relationships but overall, I just want to see my brother happy." She pinches his cheek.

He gave her a genuine smile, no tongue sticking out or a crazy face, he was happy. "And I want nothing but the same if not more for you, sis. When mom first told us of how she and dad met, your eyes were like saucers, you were captivated from the very beginning. I knew then that you would do anything to have what they do and guess what? You absolutely do and with my best friend.

Do you realize we are both dating each other's best friend?"

She shrugs, "I guess that's how we roll..." Den rolls his eyes at his sister's corniness. "You're literally the worst, sis."

Not too much later, outside on the field, Kay's

beautiful curly locks straighten and turn a dark plum as Tempest takes control. Her once ornate hazel emerald eyes change to an electric purple. She closes her eyes reciting a spell that needs all her energy, meaning she could only use it once as it drained her tremendously.

Out in front were several newbie warriors whose luck wasn't all that great as they were about to be test subjects.

Kayd decided not to use the trained warriors because the fight could come at a moment's notice.

The pups were obviously nervous, it was written all over their faces but what they endure today is nothing compared to their intense training for the next nine months.

They were standing in a fighting stance as if to approach her in a semi-circle.

The wind whips Tempest's hair around.

"Attack!"

The determined little pups shift then let out their war cry and hit top speed toward her.

She brings up her hands and then pushes them forward.

"Aliat bin lordus centan!"

A flash of amethyst and a wave of purple energy knocks them all off their feet and back into a few old redwoods. They rub their heads and backs, groaning immensely. They were so disoriented that they didn't recognize where they were or what happened for a good minute. Tempest smiled and noted that she could use that disorientation to her advantage.

"You're dismissed with a rest day tomorrow. Thank you, gentleman." Kayd announces as he turns back to his daughter, rather Tempest.

"Good job, Ka- I mean Tempest. Sorry, it took me a while to get used to Penelope too but I'm glad you're here to protect my baby girl, both you and Duchess." Tempest just smiles and nods as she listens to the internal dialogue.

D: Anything for our human. The sooner we win the sooner we can get laid!

Kay: Duchess! Really? Is that what you want to tell my father? Go to the corner!"

Duchess flounces towards the corner and sticks out her tongue.

D: See, you need relief, you're all wound up.

Kay rolls her eyes as Duchess lies on her stomach facing the wall. She can hear her humming "Please me" by Bruno Mars.

K: Very funny, Duchess!

Alpha Damien studies the Cheshire pack land. "I'll take their land and their women will be my never-ending supply of concubines. I can have a different one every night."

The excitement was clear in his voice, but Carolyn was not pleased. Though they never established what this was she always thought she was special but here he was planning to have a harem of women to satisfy his needs.

Was she not enough?

What could she do to ensure that she was the top contender for his Luna?

She never felt jealous before but now the announcement of a flood of new flesh made her aware she wasn't young and buxom anymore. The wrinkles from frustration and the constant thought of revenge, her locks becoming worn and dull, her once perky breasts needed support from a sturdy bra, and her once firm backside was practically dragging on the floor. She knew she couldn't compete; she already saw how he salivated looking at Melody's perfect cheerleader type body and how she flirted back.

She steps away as he continues blabbering on. "I know when this is over, he'll chuck me to the side, I've got to get rid of him and his son to take control. Maybe my son will help me then he can have his own pack and topple the others to the ground." Her laugh makes Damien look up, but he didn't care enough to ask.

He couldn't wait to rid himself of the Miller family and her. She had stayed way past her expiration date, he was known to toss a girl after a year or so, but Carolyn had stayed twice as long, but he was craving younger, tighter flesh.

Carolyn is startled out of her thoughts by a blood-curdling scream, "Mom! Mooooom!"

Carolyn rushes to where the voice was coming from and Brady's on the floor in the fetal position wracked in pain.

"Mom, help! Ahhhh, it hurts so much, please make it stop! Ahhhhhh!" He curls tighter as the pain seems to be getting worse. She panics and links Damien.

He approaches, looking down at a sweating, panting Brady wincing in pain on the floor.

"Hmm...guess that proves they're over."

"What do you mean? What's happening to my son?!"

He chuckles a little, "Oh, the ultimate betrayal for you see, she has gone and slept with someone else and severed the bond, it's truly over now. What a shame, I guess...now...may I get back to my planning?" He walks away as if he just reported a puff piece on the news.

"It hurts so much mom! I... AHHHH!!!!"

He was playing his role well. He had used water as sweat and tears, ripped his shirt a little and the pain? Pure acting... he was trying to prove his loyalty. If he was "betrayed" by her, nothing was keeping him loyal to her or the pack, he would be willing to tell everything to exact his revenge.

After a moment or two, he seemed to calm down, slowly getting up from the floor when she tried to help, "Don't...touch me! All physical contact hurts right now. I'm going to my room, please let me be." He clutches his stomach and limps to his room, sniffling along the way.

Melody comes in after he leaves. "What happened, who was screaming? "

"Looks like you got my son officially now, that little slut slept with someone else not too long ago. My son is all yours."

Melody is salivating, licking her lips, she finally got him, no way they could repair that relationship after her betrayal. She wanted to rip her clothes off and pounce on him right now, but Carolyn forbade it, saying he was in physical pain, severely heartbroken, and needed some time.

She agreed and when Carolyn was out of sight, she made her way into Alpha Damien's office...somebody had to scratch her itch and he was currently the man with power.

Brady flopped on his bed, pulling his burner from its secret hiding place. He had texts from the twins.

Den: I hope the plan went accordingly, sis went to visit HIM about 30 min. ago, I'm watching the security footage while she's down there.

*My <3: I miss you. Make it believable but not TOO believable! *kisses* Can't wait to be in your arms again, I love you.*

He reads hers a few more times before replying.

To Den: Yeah man, I dug deep and almost believed it myself! Phase two complete. I'll approach Damien soon to show interest. Keep my baby girl safe, bro. I'm counting on you.

To my <3: I cannot wait, I'm never letting you go! When this is over, I am whisking you away. I want to elope and later we'll plan a wedding, I won't spend another day without you being my wife. I love you dearly, baby girl."

A minute later she replies,

My <3: Anything for you, baby. I'm already yours. I'm so excited, we're getting married! I love you so much! Call me tonight, please. "

He quickly replies okay as he closes his eyes for a nap, that performance was draining but not before taking a booster of the masking potion.

Kay was taking her own potion to lessen the effects of being apart from her mate too long. It tasted like pure hot garbage.

"YUCK! They could at least make it taste good, aren't I suffering enough?!" She gags after emptying the vial into her mouth. Her mother knocks on the door.

"How are you doing, sweetie?"

She looks at her with the gag face. "I've been better." She tosses the vial in the bin and lays haphazardly across her bed and sees her mom's worried face.

"Mom, what's wrong?"

Her mom presses her hand to her face. "I'm so sorry you have to endure this; I never would have thought you would have to help me fight my battles. I'm so angry and Penelope is ready to burn them all with no time to regret it. I just want you to know how proud I am of you, Brady, and Den for coming up with a plan to end this for good."

"We just need you to finish the pack like you did last time, we'll take care of the rest. And as for continuing your fight, I don't think of it like that. There are always going to be threats for the most powerful pack in the world so bring them on! We can take them, as long as I have my family by my side."

They hug and her mom kisses her forehead, "Yeah but soon we won't be your main family, you're about to embark on a journey together with the man who loves you more than you could ever know. I still can't believe I didn't call that years ago!"

"Well, remember he was taking the mate blocker for two years, that's probably why."

"It wasn't about the drugs, Kay. His mannerisms, when he watched you, he would try to hide his smile, he found small ways to touch you especially when he was teasing you. All the signs were there...gosh, I can't believe we all missed it."

"It was just you mom; Den saw it and Trini hounded me incessantly. Speaking of shocking, what do you think about that, mom?! I knew they would make a good couple. Another opportunity I get to rub in his face. I was right!"

"Of course you will rub it in, but they are still in the beginning stages, don't rush it, let them go at their own pace. You and Brady, well, we already know where that's headed, speaking of, where is your ring?"

She walks to the beautifully ornate jewelry box and pulls it out, sliding it back on her finger. "It's the most beautiful thing I own, and I can't wait for it to be on my finger again permanently. Did I tell you we're eloping?" She puts it back in the box and closes the lid with care.

Her mom laughs, "Well it's not eloping if you tell your parents." She looks back and smiles, "Mom you know I don't keep secrets from you, and I know you love Brady, it's just that this whole ordeal is going to be major and afterward we just don't want to wait. We agreed to have a small intimate wedding later, but we can't stand not being husband and wife any longer. Please be okay with this, mom, please?" She gives her the big saucer eyes.

"Kayari, you are an adult and these decisions are yours, I wanted to do the same thing, but we also had to take into consideration my Luna ceremony but since you do not have to worry about that you can do whatever you want. You have my support and love; I just want you to be happy."

"Do they even have male Lunas?"

"I don't think that's a thing dear..."

"I hope not, he hates when I bring it up."

"But everything we do has changed the game so we could make it a thing."

"Let's not, having him as my husband and Beta is more than enough."

Her mother beams at her daughter, she had gotten that love she was searching for and was genuinely happy. Her mother prayed that they could fulfill their happily ever after.

They spend some time going over the plan again and then her mom leaves to start cooking dinner.

She lays on his pillow with her phone. This was the last call before they had to keep radio silence. "Mmm, hello my handsome husband." He couldn't help but smile. "Why hello my gorgeous wife, are you ready to finish this?"

"Most definitely. I have to be brutally honest; I miss you in ways we haven't even been together in yet." He nearly drops the phone on his face. He had to make sure they were on the same page, "What do you mean?"

She laughs, "Don't play dumb, but if you just want me to say it, I will. I want you; I need and crave you. I can't wait to have your name all over my lips." She finishes him off with a slow seductive moan of his name. At that moment he drops his phone right between his eyes.

"Owww!"

"What was that?"

"Oh baby, you made me drop my phone right on my face. It hurts now..." He rubs gingerly as he holds the phone between his jaw and shoulder.

"Oh, I'm sorry baby, I just answered your question, that's all." She laughed as quietly as she could.

"I can hear you. That was not funny." There was silence until she broke it.

"Brady, are you scared? I'm not really scared but I'll be letting Tempest loose and possibly Duchess, I guess I fear losing control."

It was new to have these powers and she didn't know how powerful she was, but Tempest did.

"Tempest and Duchess are your protectors, they wouldn't do anything to cause you harm or harm to others who don't deserve it. Trust them, it is they who will bring you back to me. I love all three of you, okay? You are the strongest entity in the world until our child is born, you wield the power to end this. Believe in yourself, I know I do."

He can hear her sniffling. "Babe, seriously? Are you crying?"

"Don't judge me right now! It's been an overly emotional day talking with mom and finding out that Den's falling for Trini and then I had to take the booster for the potion because I can't be with you right now. I just...I just wish this whole ordeal never happened and we all lived in peace and happiness, but I know it's not the real world and this has to happen. I just really miss you."

"Wow that is a lot, I'm glad to hear about Den. I knew that playboy act was a front and Trini is a special girl, not as special as mine though." She can't help but blush. "We have to endure this last part before we can do everything we want, but just remember in the end that I love you."

"And I love you, please be safe." She remembered the dream she had and told him about her fears.

"I understand but if this were to come true you can change what happens, you are so much stronger than you know. Stick to the plan and I'll be officially calling you Mrs. Preston in no time."

Her heart fluttered wildly, "I would love that."

Costume Party

The next morning Brady angrily marches down to Damien's office. He storms through the door to come face to face with him and Melody in a battle of the tongues. Melody yelps and hops off the desk about to come and explain but he holds up his hand to stop her.

"I don't care what you were doing, just get the hell out, I've got business with Damien."

He pushes her out the door without a second glance.

"Fucking slut."

Damien glares at him then smirks, "I see you've finally learned that all they're good for is a good time, now what is it that you want?" He buttons up his shirt, covering up the scratches she placed on his chest.

"I want to hurt them; I want to hurt HER. She's sleeping around like I never meant a damn thing to her and the only person getting hurt is me! I need to end her." His response was shocking and harsh, but he needed to convince him.

Damien raises his brow. "But didn't you cheat first? How are you suddenly hurt when you did what she did?"

Brady slams down his fists on the desk causing it to rattle. "Not only did she take my title from me, but she also took my best friend and everyone I knew there and turned them against me. It's not my fault I had an itch she didn't want to scratch. What else was I supposed to do? Anyway, that's not the point, she took everything from me, and I want my revenge!"

"Good, you've finally come to your senses now we just have to find a perfect time to attack."

Brady snaps his fingers and grins.

"That's it! There's a costume party this weekend. It's by invitation only so it'll be smaller than most pack parties and the costumes will hide your faces."

Damien strokes his chin, "And how do you propose we get in if it's invitation only?"

"Simple, I still have my VIP invite which includes three people." They share a laugh together.

"There may be some use for you after all. Sit down, let's discuss this party."

Den and Kay pace the stage looking out at their warriors.

"This costume party is a means to an end and though most of you will not be in attendance you will be close enough to help if needed! All guests will have an invite except our Beta who has the only VIP invite that has plus three, those assigned at the door will radio in when they arrive and tell us which costumes to be on the lookout for. After arrival, they will be looking to attack first, and we will let them."

There were a few gasps and whispers, Kay interrupts, "We want them to think they got the upper hand. When in actuality they are creating their demise. Now despite what you may have heard or thought our Beta is very much on our side, the fight and breakup was a part of the plan for him to infiltrate their house so yes, we are still together and plan on getting married after this ordeal is over."

Kayd looks shocked along with the rest of the warriors, she had told her mother but guessed she left it up to Kay to tell her father, oops!

She looks at him and mouths an apology while not breaking her strong demeanor, stepping back as Den steps forward.

"Now, does everyone understand their role in this?"

"Yes, Alpha!" The group bellowed.

They break for the day, getting their minds focused on the plan.

Den stares at her while shaking his head, "Did you really have to tell them that?"

"Do you know how many dates I've been asked out on since the breakup? Seven, it was time to nip it in the bud. Besides, they need to be focused on the task at hand, not trying to get into my pants."

"Yeah, cause nobody's getting in there!" Den laughs while running with an irate Kay right behind him.

"You're such a jerk Kamden! I'm going to kill you!"

Three days later the night of the costume party arrives. That morning, Kay lays staring at the empty side of the bed and she places his pillow against her. She scrolls through their text messages, reliving the way her heart fluttered when his special ringtone pinged that he had sent another text filled with love and hope, each one sweeter than the last.

It's been almost four days since they spoke and she was worried, he was behind enemy lines pretending to hate her, but he would be here tonight, and that part made her smile. She prayed to the Moon Goddess for protection of her pack and her family before heading to breakfast.

The kitchen was abuzz with chatter and the clinking of utensils. Mom was downstairs whipping up breakfast for the house. Kay kisses her mom and gives a stiff good morning.

"Bea, can you take over the pancakes, please?" Beatrice nods as Kam takes her daughter into the living room.

The moment they sit down Kay bursts into tears and her mom quickly takes her into her arms. "Shh shh shh, what's wrong with my baby?"

"It's everything, mom. I miss him so much, I'm nervous about this plan, and I think dad is mad at me because I didn't tell him about the elopement. I can't have daddy mad at me, I'm his princess!"

Obviously, her mom let her have her moment until her dad walks in, sitting right next to her. She looks up with big glassy eyes, finally letting them fall causing him to chuckle and kiss her forehead.

"My angel, I am not upset, you are an adult and these decisions are yours to make. You are indeed your mother's child because that's exactly what she wanted to do. You are in love and we all know love makes you do crazy things so if you want to elope princess just promise me, I get to walk you down the aisle later?"

She hugs her dad tight, feeling relieved. "Of course, daddy. I love you and I love you, mommy." Her mom joins them as they hug their baby girl, she feels comforted by the touch of her parents while still missing him.

After she gathers herself, she stands up, "Now let's get this plan into action."

Preparing

Brady analyzes his costume, "Not bad, I mean I am

going to rescue my girl, so this is appropriate." He chose
to go as Thor and though the costume was full body, he
had to continue hiding his mark and scent especially
from...

knock knock

Melody prances in wearing a genie costume, it barely
left anything to the imagination. Her only saving grace
was a micro bikini underneath.

"Hello master, it is I, your genie, coming to grant you
three wishes. Any...thing you desire, genie will do." She
bows her head and then winks.

"Wow, you look amazing." He almost choked on his lie.

She steps forward, "And you mighty Thor can ravage me
anytime. After tonight's plan we can start our own pack,
we don't need Damien."

He turns towards the mirror.

"Tell me Melody, did you think I would forget your little
tongue wrestling fest with Damien? Just how easy are

you…" He looked at her through the mirror, raising his eyebrow.

Her shoulders slump as the guilt sinks in, "It was a moment of weakness and he was so persuasive and convincing! I'm sorry baby, but once he's gone you can take over and I can be your Luna. We can grow and become even more powerful than those Millers ever were. Forgive me for my mistake baby, I swear it won't happen again." She smiles hopeful he'll forgive her faux pas with Damien though she did not mention their little romp a few days later.

She was power hungry, whomever could reign supreme is who she would bow to. She yearned to rule people, wanting them to follow her orders and work to please her. She liked Brady but if Damien won overall, she didn't mind leaving and being under him, besides, he was going to kill Carolyn or have her killed so the Luna spot was basically hers.

"It's okay, darling. Once this is over, we will discuss our roles together but for now, your sexy ass is driving me crazy! I need to keep my senses for this plan to work so I'll meet you downstairs...or we won't ever leave this room."

She squeals and puts an extra sway to her hips as she looks back, winks, and blows him a kiss. Immediately after the door closes, he scrunches up his face in disgust.

"My stomach literally cannot take another second in her presence." He shudders as he grabs his hammer and walks downstairs.

As he comes down, he notices Carolyn looking in the mirror. She's dressed as the Queen of Hearts.

Oh, how sad and pathetic, he thought.

She had to know even if he did succeed, he would never make her his Luna, he was too busy sleeping with Melody. She thought he didn't know but he overheard them one night as he went to grab a glass of water. He knew Melody only wanted to seal her role as Luna, it didn't matter who was going to be Alpha. He didn't care, he was ready for all of this to be over, he would spend the next two weeks in Kay's arms and never leave their room.

"Mother, you look nice." He laughs internally.

"Thank you, son, you look quite handsome, like your dad when he was younger."

For a moment he thought he saw a glimpse of regret in her eyes.

"But that was before he betrayed me!"

This 'betrayal' she is referring to was asking him to withdraw from his friend, Alpha Kayden and help her seek revenge and when he refused and gave her an ultimatum, she gladly walked out the door without a second thought of her husband or even her son. In actual reality, she was the betrayer and not the victim as she portrayed herself out to be.

She gathers her thoughts and calms herself. "Are you ready to exact revenge on them? Let's not forget, she betrayed you by sleeping with someone else, she stripped you of your title and humiliated you but also the fact that your aunt would be very much alive if it wasn't for her mother! Perhaps maybe we would have still been a family."

Please.

He knew she was reaching on that note but whatever convinced her. He only nodded fearing he might say what he really thought. She beamed at her son, she was so proud he finally saw her side of the story and was willing to help her exact her revenge, she never wanted to get her family back together, he had moved on with some woman he met at a bookstore, how deliciously boring, she was meant to rule not chase after her husband.

Brady was adamant on starting his own family as soon as humanly possible. He had a lot of love to give and he was going to shower his wife and their future pups, just the thought brought a smile to his face.

His mother brushes his face, bringing him back to the sad reality. "I'm so happy to see you happy about putting this plan into action, finally, the justice I seek shall be mine! My sister would be so proud of me."

Yeah, right.

Just before he could respond Alpha Damien came in wearing the King of Hearts.

Oh, this was hysterical! He was super uncomfortable, and Brady found it hilarious. Damien looks at Brady in his costume. "Why does he get to be Thor, but I have to wear this travesty? I could have been Captain America or even Iron Man."

Brady couldn't help but add insult to injury, "You guys look super cute in your couples' costume." Damien sulked but Carolyn just smiled as they waited for Melody who pranced in not too long after him, from the same direction. No wonder he was fidgeting with the zipper of his costume.

Brady scoffed internally, *What a desperate whore. Does she really think I am that dumb not to put two and two together?*

He thought as she finished readjusting her microscopic top.

Whatever, she wasn't Kayari and would never come close. He wondered what costume she had picked out.

Trini looks over her tight leotard and belt, her shield and lasso, and her wig. She dressed as Wonder Woman and Den dressed as Steve Trevor, her love interest. This would be their first formal event as a couple, Trini was thrilled when Den asked her to be his girlfriend, she had been waiting for her chance and was finally with the guy she had been crushing on since forever, now all she wanted was her best friend's happiness.

She heads to Kay's room and knocks lightly. "Come in." Trini opens the door and her mouth drops. "Oh honey, you look...wow!"

Kay dressed as the Greek goddess of Love, Aphrodite. Her white Grecian style gown was more contemporary with high slits on both sides with a waist-cinching belt and a plunging neck and backline; she draped the white shawl loosely over her arms. Her hair pinned up slightly with her crown gracing her curls.

"Thanks, all I need now is your makeup expertise. I want to look irresistible and seductive."

"You're already that, so now what?" She laughs and tells her to sit. "Alright, I will do my best, but you honey, are already gorgeous. I know what you're doing, you're trying to kill Brady with your beauty, right? You're practically torturing the man in this dress; I mean this is jaw-droppingly sexy."

She smiles, she may have picked an overly sexy costume to arouse her man but it's no fun if you don't. She shrugs her shoulders, "What can I say, I AM the Goddess of Love."

Trini starts her makeup as Den strolls in and takes notice of her costume. "Holy shit, Kay you know damn well he won't be able to concentrate with you dressed like that. He might forget the plan and just whisk you away. If that happens this is all your fault!" He lightly punches her arm and she exaggerates, screaming bloody murder,

"OWW! You heavy-handed asshole." She rubs her arm.

Twenty minutes later, her smoky eye had hints of gold, Trini applied lashes and chose a glossy rose-colored lipstick. She puts on her diamond earrings, bracelets, and armbands and lastly her Grecian style sandals. She looks in the mirror one last time and exhales loudly.

"Here we go..."

They meet her parents at the base of the stairs, Mom dressed as Poison Ivy and Dad is Batman. "Mom, you look so hot! And dad no one could be a better Batman."

He smirks, "Don't try to butter me up when you're almost naked. Who are you supposed to be?"

She smiles, "Daddy, I am Aphrodite, Goddess of Love."

He sighs, "You're going to cause that boy to lose focus..."

"HA! That's what I said, dad. He's going to completely lose focus and then we're all doomed."

She quickly punches him hard in the arm, "Payback! And he will not lose focus; this is all for the greater good. We are here to win, and I am merely playing the part."

Brady arrives with them and they wait in line, he recognizes the security as Kay's team so when he approaches, he only gives a slight nod and Knox checks his invite then nods approval. Xavier radios in that they have arrived. Kayd relays the message to the group, "Places everyone."

Kay anxiously looks for Brady but also tries to make sure she isn't too obvious. Her heart was beating wildly in anticipation, but she had to stick to the plan. She walks around speaking to the guests, welcoming them to the first official party of their title reign. There were plenty of compliments and subtle flirting, word had clearly gotten out about her huge messy breakup with Brady. She was standing by the refreshments with one of the younger Alphas from another pack.

"Perhaps another time, Christopher, my heart still has to heal before I can even think about dating again but thank you for the offer." He kisses her hand and she notices a distinct growl behind her.

"Whenever you are ready don't hesitate to give me a call, beautiful." He walks away and she rolls her eyes.

She backs into the source of the growl. "If I didn't know any better, I'd think someone was a tad bit jealous." She holds up her fan to her face to mask the conversation as she grinds into him very lightly, the sparks pulsing between them. To combat the heat rising while feeling her warm body against his, he grabs a cup from the table.

"Are you kidding, he was practically eye humping you in front of me, I'm going to add him to my kill list. On a sexier note, baby girl...that costume is deadly, you're only making this harder on yourself when I get you alone."

They lock eyes briefly and she can see the pure lust in his eyes. He winks as he looks her up and down then walks away. She leaned against the table because he was just as handsome if not more, she just wanted to be locked in a room with him, but she had a plan to execute.

Take Me to My Son!

She continues entertaining the guests, greeting others until she sees the King and Queen of Hearts costumes. She walks close to them then turns back toward her brother.

"Hey Den," She says loudly, "I'm going to check on Roman, I'll be right back." He nods, noting her new company who was eavesdropping. Feeling she was being followed, she walked towards the back of the house where the dungeon was.

She walks outside toward the entrance of the dungeon but before she could get there she's slammed against the side of the house, knocking the wind out of her. Her eyes meet with that of Alpha Damien's.

"My, my, my, what's the sweet Miller virgin doing out here by herself and in that outfit? It would be all too easy; I should have my son finish the job. I'm sure he'll have no problem with taking it. Oh wait, you gave it up already because I saw poor Brady writhing in pain on the floor, you really hurt him by becoming the slut you were meant to be. I rather enjoyed seeing him in pain though, goes to show you love doesn't exist." Alpha Damien was way too close for comfort but suddenly backed up.

"Now, take me to my son or I will gut you right here and leave pieces of your mangled body where your precious parents can find you." She tries to struggle against him but oddly he is quite strong. He grabs her by her hair forcing her in the direction of a door.

She could feel Tempest and Duchess awakening, anxious to kill, but told them to stand down as it was all part of the act, playing the vulnerable spoiled princess.

"Now, be a good little whore and open the door. Mmm, I can see why my son was so willing to take you instead of having you killed. Maybe I'll just add you to my harem once I take this wretched pack." He grabs her by her neck and forces her forward, slamming her body into the door.

When they reach the main door, he squeezes her neck hard enough for her to collapse to her knees. "Albeit a tempting offer to see what you're capable of, stop stalling and open the door!" She struggles to stand up before reaching for the key, attached to one of her bracelets. She opens the door to darkness; all the lights were removed from the hallway that led to the cells.

He growls, "I swear if you've done anything to my son,"

She cuts him off, "He deserved it if we did! I only wished I were there to witness his torture!"

She bares her teeth until he slams her against the wall then slapping her so hard, she could taste blood.

"I will not stand for your insolent tone, little girl. Final warning! Take me to my son now!"

She struggles as she leads him towards the cells, she touches her cheek which is warm to the touch, she feels the cut on her cheek. She opens the big wooden door to another dark room; he calls for him.

"Roman, son? Where are you?"

cough cough "D-dad? Is that you? Please, please get me out of here all they've done is torture and starve me...I just want to go home, dad please."

Damien lets his eyes adjust to the darkness as he approaches the sound of his voice. "Roman? Son, are you in there?" He finds an empty cot until his eyes focus on the shaking form below the small bed. Damien rushes to his son and turns Roman's body to face him. His clothes were tattered and dirty, sweat made his hair cling to his forehead and his breathing was erratic. He forces a meek smile, "Daddy..."

"Ro-" Before he could say his name Roman injected him with a substance causing him to collapse in shock. He clasps his neck in horror.

"What...what did you inject me with?!" He was angry but he couldn't shift, you could see the confusion and fear on his face.

Any werewolf will tell you the idea of being unable to shift is their worst nightmare.

Roman towers above his father, acting perfectly normal. He slicks his hair back out of his face and smirks.

"Finally, the tables have turned, now who's shaking in fear? I only wish mom were here to see this. Remember her?! The woman who loved you unconditionally but all you did was leave her bloody and battered calling her worthless, a whore, a slut, oh, and my personal favorite, just another piece of ass? Well, I remember every ill syllable you spoke to my mother and I vowed to get my revenge at any cost."

"TRAITOR!" He tries to lunge at him but not only does the injection keep him from shifting, it makes him weak. It's getting harder for him to breathe as he pulls his weak frame against the nearest wall.

Roman scoffs at his effort. "Oh, what's the matter, father? Now you know what it feels like when someone you trust betrays you. You hurt her so much and I had to watch her try to put on a facade for me so that I wouldn't worry about her. She would continue to make dinner with her black eyes, her bruises, and broken ribs, wiping the blood off the counter from her busted lip, just to give me the tiniest bit of normalcy, but did you care?! No, you were only worried about yourself and the next set of legs you could get in between. I WAS THERE! The moment you slept with someone else and mom was doubled over in searing pain, it broke me, it broke me so much to see her like that and to know it was you causing it. That was the moment I vowed to stop her suffering and I told her I would end you so she would never have to look over her shoulder in fear again."

Tears streamed down Roman's face as he recalled all the horrible moments of his childhood. His mother was his saving grace, she raised him to not be anything like his father.

"Son, j-just please, I know I made mistakes, but I can fix them, I swear! Just give me a chance!"

Roman laughs hysterically at his pathetic groveling, it reverberates through the halls. "BEG for your worthless life! That's what you made mom do before you viciously beat her, I didn't know if that day was her last because you beat her worse than the time before. I will make sure you suffer these last moments of your life and I sure as hell won't miss you."

Damien is shocked listening to his son drain all his emotion but the clearest one is disappointment.

"You are the worst father a child could ask for, I wish I wasn't your child and I will never tell my kids about the monster who gave me life, I wish your vile blood didn't run through my veins, I wish my mother never loved such a pathetic excuse for a man. Goodbye *Damien*, know that my only regret is that I didn't do this sooner."

Terror grips Damien's eyes, "What are you going to do?!" There's fear in his voice as he watches his son shift into his wolf, Aeracles.

Aeracles stood quite tall for a wolf and his fur was silver. A silver wolf was super rare, and Kay was in awe of his haunting beauty. Roman's eyes turn to an icy sapphire blue before he gives her the signal then turns back to his father, approaching him slowly like any predator approaches its wounded prey.

Kay turns around as she cringes from the blood curdling screams coming from his unlocked cell until there was no more screaming. She could hear bones crunching and she started to walk a bit faster as Roman said he would take his time ending his father's life.

Kay vs. Melody

As she heads upstairs to their room, she's startled
to see Brady waiting there, he was on her side holding
her pillow and inhaling her scent, her heart melted but
when he saw her injuries, he almost lost control, Raven
was irate, screaming to find out who harmed his mate.

*Raven: Who. the. fuck?! I swear human you better find
out who did this, or I WILL! NOBODY TOUCHES HER
LIKE THAT!!! I want their blood, I want their screams, I
want their soul!*

There was no calming him down and honestly, Brady
didn't want to, Raven was livid, his anger boiled like
lava, but he couldn't react so drastically, or he could ruin
the whole plan.

Brady closes his eyes and takes a few breaths as Kay
heads to the bathroom. She surveys the damage which
was minimal because Alphas heal quicker than normal
wolves. By now she was only spitting out the remaining
blood, but she had already healed. Brady, now back in
control, leans against the door frame with his arms
crossed, still quite pissed.

"Don't worry, he's very much dead. Roman took care of that, see I told you he was an asset." He growls at his name then shrugs, "He may have helped but he's still my enemy, I will never trust someone who threatens something like that, he's despicable. Now, to kill my mother."

She places her hands on his chest, "Baby, let someone else do it or you'll regret it for the rest of your life, and I don't want you to live with that guilt."

He takes both of her hands and kisses them. "No, this is my battle, being with her these past few days proved to me just how weak she has become. She's just another filthy rogue as far as I'm concerned."

It broke her heart to see his inner turmoil with his own mother. No child wants to even think of killing a parent but here it was the easiest decision of the whole plan. She couldn't even imagine how he was feeling.

Her hand caresses his face, her touch and scent calming him down. She leans forward for a kiss, but he backs away, she looks heartbroken until he explains "Baby, if I start, I promise you I will not stop, rain check, especially in that." He kisses her forehead before looking her over once more. "I need the strength of the Moon Goddess to not lock you in here right now."

She blushes as she pushes him out the door and back to the party. "Stick to the plan, sir."

Over link the security team reported a large mass moving just outside the pack border. It could only be Damien's "pack". Kayd orders border patrol to stand down and come back to HQ to let them think they are busy with the festivities and unaware of the imminent attack.

Meanwhile, Kay finds her parents and her brother. She's not showing any sign of the struggle from earlier, so she refrains from going into detail. "Roman has taken care of *Alpha* Damien."

Carolyn searches for Damien but ends up running into Melody, she had no reason to be cordial anymore they were vying for the same title.

"Have you seen Damien; he hasn't returned from the dungeon."

Melody watches all the males in costume licking her lips hungrily. "Maybe you can allow a son and father some time alone? Perhaps Damien is relaying the plan to his son."

Carolyn notices her eyes roaming, "Didn't you just get my son in your grasp and here you are ready to play leapfrog? I guess you really can't turn a whore into a housewife."

Melody eyes her up and down, laughing. "I know you're not stupid Carolyn, you know about Damien and me, I'm playing the field to increase my chances of becoming Luna whether it be Damien, Brady, or even Roman. It's not about the man, it's about the power and they won't be able to resist what I have to offer. The best you can be is what you already are, a chew toy to play with whenever he feels like it, but this young, supple body and all my... *talents* will land me on the throne." Melody licks her lips and pushes up her boobs before sauntering away as one of the men catches her attention.

Brady watches Kay from the refreshment table talking to a couple of males. His face is distorted in disgust. Melody places her hand on his shoulder. "Don't worry baby...she'll get what's coming to her soon...Let's have a little fun, how about we make her a bit jealous?"

Before he could respond she pulls him down for a kiss just as Kay's eyes look in their direction. She gasps and drops her glass; it shatters causing a silence as everyone looks at her looking at him.

Tears streamed down her face as her lip started to quiver. He wraps his arms tightly around Melody to enhance the effect, but his stomach was begging to empty its contents. He unlocks their lips and forces a smile as he gazes at her, "Mmm, you naughty naughty girl..."

She smiles and watches as Kay walks away quickly trying not to let anyone see her upset. "I'm not done with the Princess yet; I'm going to rid the world of that spoiled brat especially after she assaulted me that morning. I'm going to enjoy watching her take her final breath."

Kay sits outside in tears, she knew it was an act, but she still felt hurt and betrayed. She sniffled and wiped her face before she heard the breaking of a branch...and then another and another. Before she knew it, Alpha Damien's followers surrounded her. They were a massive bunch, no one stood less than six-foot-tall, and their presence was very intimidating. Half of them shifted to their wolf and the others had weapons. As they encircled Kay, she stood up trying frantically to find an escape route, but it was useless, she was surrounded. She linked her mother and told her what was happening.

One of the men spat out, "This must be her, Alpha Damien said she was...pure." He licks his lips and suddenly she feels uneasy.

"Don't...touch her! She's mine." Melody shoves through the group of warriors. She stops in the middle of the circle standing close to Kay.

"How does it feel? Hmm? To lose everything. I hope you know I have enjoyed Brady every...single...night since that morning of your breakup and he is amazing in bed." She licks her lips and twists them up in an evil smirk.

That lying bitch.

Kay laughs internally. "Of course he would, it's just *so* easy coming from the likes of you. What do you want Melody? Still bitter about me body-slamming you in the kitchen. Are you going to sic your little pack on me to do your dirty work for you?"

She steps closer, "Oh no honey your death will be by my hands and no one else's. My men are here to dispose of your worthless pack and family."

Kay knew she only had one shot as she waited for her mom to give her the signal that they were ready.

Kay laughs to the point that everyone is looking at her, questioning her sanity. Melody steps back cautiously, not knowing what she might do. Kay is in a stomach cramping guffaw. Her laugh slows down, and she wipes a tear from her eye.

"Oh Melody, you stupid whore. You're a terrible liar, you know that? I know that Brady hasn't touched you besides that little display you just put on for me. Bravo!" She does a slow clap, her mom signals that they're ready as she continues. "But you see Melody, there is something I should confess..."

She steps closer and closer until she's mere centimeters from her ear.

"Are you listening dear? Good... I am going to enjoy destroying you."

She steps away and her once curly locks cascade down and become that deep purple that signals Tempest taking control, her fiery amethyst eyes focus on Melody who looks shocked as Kay lifts her arms, reciting that spell she had practiced on the pups.

The wind whips her long flowing locks around before she brings her arms down with force.

"Aliat bin lordus centan!!!!"

A pulse of purple energy moves forward swiftly, knocking them all off their feet as she screams the force out of her body. When she drops her arms, she is panting on her knees, momentarily weak but regaining her strength as her mother had taught her.

She focuses on recovering quickly, "Moon Goddess give me the strength I need to beat my enemies, the strength I need to protect what is mine, the strength I need to protect my family!"

She shakily stands up as she looks at the mass of bodies writhing on the ground. They shake their heads vigorously trying to figure out what just happened. Melody shakes her head wildly as she is dazed by this turn of events. She stands still regaining her balance, her face twisted up in rage.

"NO! You couldn't have gained your powers! You weren't marked! How did you..."

Kay sits back on the log pondering her question, "Well, Melody, they say there's a pill for everything, energy, male impotency, weight loss... there's even one to mask your mate scent and mark. Best believe I had him mark me as soon as we learned about the plot against our pack. You see this was all a fake, the argument, the breakup, him running to his mother, him running to the likes of YOU! That man is all mine and I'll have him in OUR bed before they can properly bury you. Bet you're wondering how?"

As she goes to explain, Penelope bursts through the patio doors, the storm clouds forming quickly over the territory as she reaches to the sky to gather the lightning that was showering from above. Her mother's hair was a stunning violet and her eyes matching the intensity. She screeches as the lightning surrounds her body; she collects it in a ball of energy. She hurls the force field before launching the ball towards Melody, but Kay uses her power to knock Melody out of the path of destruction so that the ball of energy envelops the pack.

The men stand frozen in fear, not knowing what to do or how to escape the force field as they watch her. Penelope smirked evilly, the black vines creeping across her body as she recites the same spell that rid her of John Michael's pack of fools. She winks and the flames and lightning envelop the men. The screams were nightmare worthy as they were both electrocuted and burned alive until...silence.

"You think I'm going to run because your

mommy got rid of my warriors?! Well, you're wrong, I swear I am going to kill you and her!" She shifted into her wolf, which was blonde and had yellow eyes. She was an average-sized wolf and Alpha wolves were larger, but it didn't matter, her hatred towards Kay was greater than her sense.

Kay watches as Melody paces back and forth before she lunges at her. "Stop it, Melody, save yourself, fair warning!" Kay could feel Duchess scratching the surface.

"If it's the last thing I do I will destroy your precious world!" Melody shifted back and threw a blade she had hidden in her costume in the direction of Kay's family who was watching. Kay's instincts couldn't react quickly enough to do anything but scream.

"NO!!!"

She heard a grunt before she could turn around. When she does, she sees her beloved collapsing, he had jumped in front of her parents. Brady gasps as he looks down in shock to see the knife lodged into his chest, almost dead center. Out of pure adrenaline, he yanks it out, but it was too late, the blade coated in wolfsbane was already coursing through his system. He was pale and sweaty as he fell to the ground. Kay tries to run to him, but Melody comes behind her with a second blade, scratching it against the sensitive skin on her neck as it moves along with her breathing rhythm. "Move another inch and I'll slit your throat!"

Kayd and Den tended to Brady who was breathing shallowly as his eyes met hers, there was fear in them as he tried to speak. "I...I l-love you." He whispers as his eyes close and his body goes limp.

"BRADY! No, baby, please!" She collapses to the ground as she watches her dad try to shake him to respond.

"Oops, guess I aimed a bit too high, oh well. He was pathetic to keep pining after you anyway. I was right there willing to give him everything he wanted." She laughs wickedly as Kay drowns in tears unable to focus, the entire world had stopped, she was in a dark place. She had lost her love, the very reason for fighting, and she didn't think she could go on without him, in fact, she was waiting for that excruciating pain of a broken bond, but it didn't happen. She looked over and he was still alive, barely, as he coughed and slowly opened his eyes. He struggled to turn his head to meet her eyes and smile, but he needed to see her.

She felt a surge of energy as the pack doctor tended to him. She stands up and faces off against Melody, her hair whipping around as the wind picks up.

"You're going to pay for trying to kill my fiancé. I'm going to rip your heart out and shove it down your throat!"

Melody quickly throws the blade in her hand, but it bounces off the purple force field surrounding Kay as it falls to the ground. Again, Melody shifts back into her wolf. Kay closes her eyes calling forth both Duchess and Tempest.

K: I have never felt this much rage before, I'm shaking in anger. I want her death to be unlike any other. I want her to suffer considerably, I want to make her an example and see the fear in her eyes moments before she dies! I am giving up my control to whoever thinks they can make her suffer the most.

D: Don't worry I talked about this with Penelope, we...umm...learned something that we agreed to do only in extreme circumstances, and I believe this counts when that bitch just tried to kill our mate. I want nothing but her eternal suffering!

T: I agree, let's do this! Don't be afraid, we will take care of her in the most vicious way.

"Stop fucking stalling!" Melody bares her teeth in impatience.

Kay slips into her subconscious as Duchess takes over. Duchess was considered small for a female Alpha wolf, she growled as her beautiful white fur stood straight up. She didn't have the distinct ring around her eye like her dad and brother did, but her fur was so white it was close to a platinum white, a beautiful oddity. Duchess' whole body shivers and as soon as her eyes open, they are that amethyst purple as when Tempest is in control.

They all gasp, Kayd looks at Kam as the doctor tends to Brady, giving him an antibody shot to help speed up his healing process.

"Baby doll, what's happening to our little girl?"

Kam stands slowly with her mouth wide open, "She's done it, I've heard it could be done but I've never seen it...she's harnessed the power of both her wolf and her witch at the same time, it's...it's never been done by a Legacy! Until now..."

Duchess growls as her eyes glow brighter, "Last chance to walk away with your life, Melody. The fact that you almost tried to kill our fiancé is enough to snap your neck but Kay's tired of all the bloodshed and so for her, we are going to offer this once. Leave now and live or stay to die a painful death."

Melody snarls before she lunges towards Duchess, sinking her teeth into her back-left leg, trying to inflict as much pain as she could. Duchess yelps but manages to swing her leg, launching Melody into a tree hitting with a vicious thud.

"Very well then." The purple glow amplifies around her wolf. Melody is frozen in place as Duchess runs full speed towards her. She hits her with a sickening thud causing her to become airborne before she hits the ground hard, whimpering. Her wolf lies there for a moment.

Duchess stalks her prey as Melody desperately tries to attack her again but Duchess/Tempest's eyes glow, suspending Melody in the air. Melody struggles to break the hold, enraged she couldn't do anything.

"You haven't won! As long as there are rogues, you'll always be fighting to keep your power! You will never be safe, you will never not be looking over your shoulder, you will always be on guard because the Cheshire pack will fall! Mark my words!"

Kay closes her hand to restrict Melody's airflow. All Melody could do was gasp, she shifts back in panic as she clutches her throat, panting for the tiniest bit of air. She's still suspended in the air as Kay shifts back but Duchess and Tempest are still in control, her hair long and flowing, her eyes burning amethyst.

"That's fine, we're okay with fighting for our pack, fighting for our family, and most importantly fighting for love. What we're not okay with is some rogue whore trying to infiltrate our pack and take everything from me because she went along with a psychotic bitch who wants to destroy my mother. Now your fate will be the same as Damien's, a slow torturous death!"

Melody's eyes widened when she heard of Damien's demise.

"Oh, have you not wondered why you couldn't find the bastard or why he hasn't come to save you? His son took care of him, it was music to my ears to hear his ear-piercing screams." Tempest laughs slowly.

Tempest takes her shock as a moment to check on Brady. His healing was terribly slow due to the poison and his complexion still pale and for that Tempest's rage flared up all over again.

She turns back and clenches her hand tighter, closing Melody's windpipe more. How easy it would be to just crush it and end it all, but she wanted her to suffer.

Tempest tilts her head as she releases the force field and Melody drops hard to the ground. Tempest walks up to her and crouches down.

"What's the matter, huh? What happened? Answer me! You tried to kill me, my family, my love! Fight! Fight for your miserable, pathetic, worthless life so I can end it!"

Tempest's chest heaves in anger as she watches Melody struggle for a simple breath. She wanted her to suffer, suffer so much that her death will be an example to others who even think to cross their pack.

"Baby girl..." A soft voice whispers to her and suddenly she's back in control as she looks over to Brady leaning on his elbows still breathing hard.

Wolfsbane attacks the respiratory system causing panic which doesn't allow the victim to shift. From there it slowly breaks down vital organs until the heart stops, if not treated quickly with an injection, death is inevitable.

Brady had almost healed, but he was still fighting the effects of the poison. He can see the rage and fury in her now distinguishing green/hazel eyes, but she walks over while holding her hand closed, keeping Melody's airflow restricted. His touch was gentle, his smile melted her heart as the tears formed and fell down her cheeks.

"You end this. End this now, my love..." He kisses her hand.

She looked at him surprised! She thought he would be the voice of reason, talk her out of it, spare Melody's life, lock her away in the dungeon for good. But he knew that it was a temporary fix to a permanent problem, she had to end it like he still had to confront his mother.

He places his hand on her face and her eyes instantly close feeling his warmth, his love.

Let Me...

"**Y**ou you'll ne-never win! Your pack will fail! This miserable family has more enemies than it knows, someone will succeed!"

He gazes at Kay and nods; she smiles warmly at him. She stands up and her hair is amethyst again, whipping around fiercely as the clouds form all around once more. Everyone is mesmerized by the cloud-to-cloud lightning.

"So long Melody, it was never a pleasure..."

Kay reaches skyward and the lightning envelops her until a fireball appears in her hand, she smirks as she puts all the anger, the hate, the frustration and all the negativity into the sphere, it turns black, all the malice swirling around in its dark void. She shrieks as she hurls it towards her at an alarming speed. Instead of engulfing her body in electrical torture and burning her to cinders the ball shoots through her chest and explodes the tree behind her as her body crumples to the ground. Her eyes are wide open as she lies on her side, her chest has a huge burning hole about the size of a baseball where her cold heart once was.

Trini screams but Den pulls her into him, so she doesn't have to see the horrific scene, even he cringed a little.

Kay collapses, breathing hard. It was over and the first thing she felt was the sparks and tingles as she recognized his touch.

"Baby...are you okay?" He smiles, she wraps her arms around him tightly as if he would disappear at any moment.

"I'm okay baby girl, just lethargic. Doctor says I just need some bed rest for a few days and luckily, I have the perfect nurse to take care of me." He gives her a small smile as he leans in for the kiss he's been waiting for all night. He pulls back to see the brightest smile on her face.

"I missed you."

"I missed you too, I told you that you could do it. It was crazy to see your wolf and your witch combine! It was badass!" He smiles as he kisses her forehead, but she frowns.

"What about your mother? She got away." They had completely forgotten about Carolyn and she was either hiding or had run. Kayd links the grounds to see if anyone had seen her.

"I got her right here!" Roman harshly throws Carolyn on the ground in front of them, his face and clothes still smeared in his father's blood. Brady growls as he meets Roman's eyes.

"Hey! Now is not the time, baby. Focus!"

Brady sends a glare Roman's way to signal that this wasn't over as he shifts his eyes to his so-called mother.

Carolyn looks up to see Brady with Kayari and scoffs, "I should have known...just like your father...I don't regret leaving you! You're weak and pathetic, you think this will last? It won't, she'll break your heart and you deserve it for being so stupid!"

Now it was his turn to laugh, "No, Carolyn because she put together my heart after you shattered it. You're so stupid, do you not get it? AUNT. BRIDGET. WAS. A. WHORE! Any woman willing to kill innocent babies should die a thousand deaths." He laughs as he stalks her, still reeling from the poisoning but relishing in her vulnerability, he had no reason to hold his tongue.

"She was weak for dick and you're the same, tell me, did you actually think Damien would make you his Queen? You're a blind fool if you didn't know he was screwing Melody behind your back. Did you know he planned to have you killed when he won, I saw it in the plans he stupidly wrote down? He was going to slice you from ear to ear with a silver laced dagger."

"You're lying! Damien loved me! We may not be like *them*," She spat as she pointed to Kayd and Kam, "but there was something there."

"Yeah, delusion! He planned to kill you and me so he and Melody could reign together, you were just a sad used up liability. You were *his* whore!" He pants in anger. "And you were my nightmare...How could you abandon your own child and husband? HOW?!" He was in shambles, tears streaming down as he looked at the woman who birthed him.

She looks him dead in the eye, "You were a mistake. I wish I never birthed such a pitiful excuse of a son. You mean nothing to me, just another enemy of me and my sister..."

"Enough!" Kam raises her hand and Carolyn is gasping for air. She steps forward as Kay pulls Brady into a hug; he's reeling from her harsh words. Kam stands in front of a gasping Carolyn.

"Don't you dare speak to him like that, the mistake here is you! I will not allow you to scar such a strong and caring boy with a bright future ahead of him. How he was able to show love after suffering so long with the likes of you is nothing short of a miracle. He could have been bitter, lashed out, and closed himself off but he didn't, and a friendship blossomed into love like no other. Their love is more special than my husband and I's. What they have gone through so far ensures that what they have is going to last. All your sister wanted to do was hurt me and why? Because she thought I had an interest in getting back with John Michael after I told her repeatedly that I didn't, she was just bitter she was rejected by him, twice. And the moment she threatened my children I had no qualms about incinerating her into a pile of ash on the ground."

Brady rushes over as quickly as he could to Kam, "Mrs. Miller, no, let me do this, she's my problem."

She holds his hand and smiles. "Son, I will not let you live with the burden of killing your mother. I want your happiness with my baby girl, focus on the love you two share, the children you will raise, the family you deserve. Do not let her win! This is a long-seeded war and it started with me, not you. Trust me when I say everything she has said is a lie, anyone with a heart can see your worth and my daughter is head over heels in love with you, go and be by her side, let me finish this as a favor to you and know that I am so proud to call you my family."

His tears are now of joy as he feels the love radiating from her, it was pure, it was genuine, and he knew she was right. This would affect him greatly if Carolyn fell by his hands, no matter how much he hated her she was still his mother.

Kam wipes the tears from his cheek, "Please." He looks back at Carolyn who seems unbothered by all the emotion between her enemy and her son.

Suddenly it dawned on him, he felt what he had been wanting to for all these years, absolutely nothing. He was void of any feeling towards her and he finally smiles at the revelation.

He looks at her then hugs Kam, kissing her cheek. "Thank you, mom."

Carolyn clicks her tongue, screaming, "Your family has taken everything from me! My king, my son, and my pack but more importantly you took my sister from me! How can you live with yourself knowing that?"

"How can I?! How could she had she succeeded in killing me and my children?! I'd tell you to seek help, but you won't be living that long to find it. And for the record, you walked away from your husband and son to shack up with someone to dispose of you like a trash bag. Even after you left Brady, he still loved you and longed for you, all he wanted was his mother to love him, to encourage him, to just be there. How do you feel about him calling Gracie, and now me, mom? Does that even bother you?"

Carolyn looks at Brady, he doesn't look back, he's distracted by Kayari pulling his face in her direction, he smiled as she whispered to him and he nodded. She pulls him into the house without another word or so much as even a glance from him, he is done.

Our Night

Kayari pulls Brady into their room, closing and
locking the door behind her. "No need to lock me in. I'm
not going anywhere, in fact, we're not going anywhere
for at least a week. I've missed you so much."

She turns around, her costume molded to her perfectly
with her legs peeking out from the side splits, even after
all the fighting she managed to still look ravishing. For a
few moments, they just stare at each other until he
shakes out of his daze.

"Wow, how did I get so lucky?"

She could feel the heat radiating off her cheeks. "I
should count myself the lucky one, to have someone
caring, supportive, and willing to do anything to make
sure I'm happy. Now, if he could refrain from dying on
my watch that would make my life a little easier." She
grins as she saunters over to him. His hands gently
placed on her hips and hers around his neck.

"To be fair, I didn't know she was going to try and kill
me." He chuckles but tears form, and Kay starts to cry,
the adrenaline and fighting finally hit her, she had almost
lost him.

"Hey, hey, hey, I'm here and I am fine. All I want is to lock myself away with you and never let you go."

She leans against the bedpost then they stare at each other, she eyes him up and down, playfully biting her lip. No words were needed as he slowly approached her.

Step by step, drowning her in anticipation as her breath quickens.

He steps closer, he can see her eyes dilate into pools of lust.

Closer, she smiles before she's back to her seductive pout. He missed those soft lips on his.

Closer, he places his hands around her waist, slowly.

She couldn't take the teasing as she slammed her lips into his, running her fingers in his hair pulling roughly. He groans, she knew that it was his weakness. In response, he picks her up and she wraps her legs around him. She realizes they're not headed towards their bed.

She looks at him in question. "I'm running us a bath. You grab our clothes and order room service to be here in an hour. He sets her down, smacking her on the ass.

Damn, he missed that.

She squeals as she goes into their closet.

He runs the bath adding lots of lavender and mint. Her favorite artist comes over the speakers, loud enough to fill their room as well.

As he watches the tub fill, he can't help but go over all the events of the past couple of weeks.

They were a day into power and war was waged against them by his own family. No, she wasn't family, just someone he knew, nothing more. There was the discovery of a mole and they worked tirelessly to create a plan to weed out all the pack traitors, luckily it was just the one.

Then his heart started to beat fast as he remembered her kidnapping.

One of the worst moments of his life. He was still conflicted with Roman, although he helped by providing vital information then killing Damien and catching Carolyn, he had still threatened to physically assault the girl he loved and that made his blood boil all over again. He didn't realize he had been balling his hands into fists until she called out.

"Shorts or pajama bottoms?" If it were up to him, they'd be wearing nothing but since she ordered food he replied, "Basketball shorts."

Easier to remove, he thought.

He wasn't stupid he knew the moment they were out of this bath she would have her way with him. They may have no experience with sex, but the tension could be felt anywhere. But before they shared their first time, he wanted to right a wrong.

She strolls in with his red basketball shorts and her pajamas were hidden under his, piquing his curiosity. He leans over her shoulder, pressing soft kisses to her neck and shoulders while trying to see what it was. She pushed him back slightly as she put her clothes under her towel.

"No peeking...now, help me out of this dress...please."

She leans forward placing her hands on the counter. He tried to focus on the zipper while staring at her open back where her dress dipped to right above the small of her back. Her legs peeking out from the splits of her dress, she was practically naked all night.

He growls, "I just realized you've been almost naked all night." His hands roamed up her hips to feel fabric and he sighs in relief. He looks at her and she is not happy, baring her teeth as Duchess was offended, "Of course I'm wearing underwear, I'm not crazy."

He leans in, squeezing his arms around her, kissing her temple. "I'm sorry to have even thought that I just didn't want anyone to touch you or take advantage." She rolls her eyes as they return to normal and turns around, still in his grasp. "This was for you and only you besides, you saw what happens when someone pisses me off."

"But Damien..."

"That was for him to let his guard down, to think I was vulnerable. To him, I was just the Miller virgin. It took everything in me to not rip him apart after he slapped me. Tempest was not too happy."

T: Still not! That bastard had some nerve!

D: I wanted him as a snack! I could have helped Aeracles, ripping him in half, then quarters. Then feasting on his fear! THAT would have sustained me.

She chuckles at the inner dialogue. "Anyway, I'm glad it all worked out and you didn't have to..."

He places his finger across her lips "Shhh, no more talk. I need those lips for other things."

She pulls up her hair as he unzips and slides it down her curves until it pools on the floor.

He takes a moment to appreciate the woman in front of him. He could hear Raven growling.

R: Finally mate all ours.

He wasn't a wolf of many words.

H

e's brought out his thoughts when she clears her

throat. He looks at her through the mirror. She scrawls "KDMP loves BMP" in the mirror steam. He takes her hands and leads her into the tub before he undresses. She watched him like a hungry bear, she was licking her lips before he cleared his throat jolting her eyes upward.

He smiles. "Like what you see?" He knew she wouldn't answer; she merely looked away, but he could see the corners of her mouth turned upward. The water was piping hot and he had to ease in, unlike her who sank in with a sigh of relief. This is why they didn't shower together, he felt like he was being water tortured while she basked in the hot water. Right now, he felt like a tea bag, steeped and ready for consumption.

The moment after he was fully submerged and sighed in relief, she turned around and lay against him, the sparks and tingles flowing freely between them and it was magical. The first jolt causes a moan to fall from her lips causing him to shift a bit. She looks down and smiles, "Already? Hmmm...this is going to be fun." She bathes him and he bathes her before he wraps himself in a towel and reaches for hers, opening it up so she could step in. He wraps her in the towel, rubbing her down to dry her off. He then puts on his basketball shorts and at that moment room service knocks on the door.

He kisses her cheek, "I'll get it."

She smiles as she finds her favorite essential oil and rubs herself down in it before putting on her lace boy shorts and crop cami with lace detail, the set was a burgundy red, his favorite color. She finishes by washing her face and turning off the lights.

"Hey, I ordered easy stuff like burgers, fries and pizza. I hope that's..." He turns around and his jaw drops. She was wearing next to nothing but next to nothing in his favorite color and she looked beautiful beyond words. She walks past him to her side of the bed, sitting where her arms accentuated her breasts more. "So... you like? I bought this when I bought the gold dress. It was the only set in your favorite color, so I called it fate for me to buy it...just...for...you."

He growls as he pulls her against him, "Oh, baby you have no idea...but first..." He takes her to the vanity, he faces her taking her hands, kissing each finger, each one receiving its own special attention.

"Where did you put your ring?"

Her face lights up as she remembers that she could wear it again. She reaches into her jewelry box to put it on, but he stops her. She looked confused as he took it from her hand.

"I want to do this again because there's so much more to be thankful for so..." He takes her hand and drops to one knee, she gasps as if it was the first time, her eyes already producing tears.

"Kayari Denise Miller, love of my life, protector of my heart and absolutely the best thing that could ever happen to me, please grant me the honor to be able to call you Mrs. Preston for the rest of my life. Will you marry me, my sweet baby girl?"

She clutches her hand over her mouth trying to mute her cries long enough to answer but she was just so overwhelmed. He lets her run through the gamut of emotion as she bends down to hug him, his arms wrap tightly around her. A minute or two later she stands while he still holds her hand. She takes a deep breath, "Yes, Brady, yes I'll marry you. I'm yours forever and ever." She breaks down into his arms after he slips the ring back on her finger.

He places his hand on her cheek pulling her in, "I've been waiting so long for this moment and nothing is more important than my beautiful girl in front of me." She blushes and smiles. His thumb traces her lips before leaning down for a kiss. She bites her lip, "I need you, Brady, please." He nods as he lays her on their bed finally having their moment together.

AHEM The Final Showdown

"*H*i guys, Kayari here. Bet you're wondering

just what happened to Carolyn? You were probably like:

'NO! That was the best part! I mean, I'm glad you guys are back together and all, but I REALLY wanted to see that bitch die.'

Well, let me warn you...it isn't pretty ladies and gentlemen but...read on."

RECAP: He looks at her then hugs Kam, kissing her cheek. "Thank you, mom."

Carolyn clicks her tongue, screaming, "Your family has taken everything from me! My king, my son, and my pack but more importantly you took my sister from me! How can you live with yourself knowing that?"

"How can I?! How could she had she succeeded in killing me and my children?! I'd tell you to seek help, but you won't be living that long to find it. And for the record, you walked away from your husband and son to shack up with someone ready to dispose of you like a trash bag. Even after you left Brady, he still loved you and longed for you, all he wanted was his mother to love him, to encourage him, to just be there. How do you feel about him calling Gracie, and now me, mom? Does that even bother you?"

PRESENT:

"Why should I care, he turned his back on me just like his worthless father."

"Are you kidding me? He did it for his own sanity! Repeatedly he tried to find some semblance of his mother from when he was little, the Carolyn I thought I knew too, but it was all a scheme wasn't it? All he found was a bitter, vindictive old fool! You want vengeance for your sister? Then make your move."

Carolyn laughs, "No way, you'll just use your magic powers and I'll have no chance of winning. I want a fair fight, no other powers, just your wolf."

Kam sighs, "Fair enough, Carolyn."

Kayd quickly pulls her aside, "Are you kidding me, you expect me to watch you fight? No way, let me do this, it's because of my brother that this all started."

He was hesitant because Kam's wolf, Tatiana, wasn't as combat-ready as Penelope and thus weaker.

"I know you're worried, but she can do this, trust me. Promise me you won't interfere?" She hears him growling in protest. "Kaydy... promise me."

He lost all fight after she spoke his pet name. "Fine, but I won't hesitate to send Trini after her if you're in any trouble, you're lucky our baby girl is occupied at the moment." He shakes his head not wanting to think about what could be happening.

Kam chuckles at his uneasiness, "Our little girl is basically married much like we were, deal with it, honey."

He rolls his eyes and smiles before his face turns serious again. "Just please be careful, that goes for you, too." He looks beyond Kam to Penelope and Tati.

Tati hadn't had as much practice or training as Penelope, her witch was obviously the dominating trait, but Kam would let Tati roam from time to time.

Tati was a beautiful onyx wolf, her fur so dark it had a purple tint that marked her family's Legacy line. She also had piercing dark grey eyes, her combination also a rarity. Kam could hear Tati talking to Penelope.

P: You can beat her but fair warning if she pulls anything sneaky, I'm taking control and vaporizing the bitch.

T: I know, I will gladly let you take over but for now...she's mine.

Tati growls as she looks at Carolyn who had shifted into her wolf, nothing special just the average looking brown wolf, and her eyes were black. She paces as Kam looks at Kayd who kisses her forehead. "Good luck, baby doll."

Kam shifts and Tati appears, standing tall. Carolyn takes no time lunging at Tati clamping down on her shoulder.

Tati yelps at the pain and collapses a little. Then she recovers and is back on all fours as she pushes Carolyn towards a tree. She slams her against the tree causing Carolyn to let go of the death grip on her shoulder.

Carolyn growls in response, lunging for Tati's legs. Tati jumps out of the way, putting some distance between them, checking the damage done. Her shoulder was healing slowly. She felt okay to continue.

Kayd could feel Phoenix itching to surface, but he had to let her fight her battles. Of course, he would help his beloved but that's not what she requested of him and he had to step aside despite his objection.

Kamden also anxiously watched his mother fight; he was against her bringing out Tati just because she was more powerful in her witch. "Dad, I don't like this, what if she gets hurt? Trinity, be ready to come in if she doesn't fight fair." Trini's wolf, Iliana, begins to stir.

I: More than happy to, anything for my mother-in-law.

Though they hadn't discussed their next steps, Trini knew she was head over heels in love with Kamden. She knew he loved her in some capacity though he hadn't said the big three, she was in no rush really, she already had him, and their relationship would blossom. Trini moves to the side to see the fight better.

Carolyn was now on top of Tati, growling and baring her teeth, inching down closer and closer. She was trying to clamp down on Tati's throat and end this quickly, but Tati caught on putting her front paws up while trying to get her legs underneath.

Once she does, she pushes up and launches her to the far side of the lawn. Carolyn yelps as she stands up and is now limping. When she fell, she landed on her hind legs, more so on her left leg causing a sharp pain to shoot up her spine.

She whimpered then her face turned up in a rage, she let out a vicious roar as her black eyes now bored a hole through Tati, who was anxious for her next move.

Suddenly, Carolyn shifts back and instantly pulls a knife from behind her, throwing it right at Tati!

Tati isn't quick enough to dodge the blade and lurches back as it lodges into her chest and she collapses. Kamden can barely hold his dad back from totally ripping Carolyn apart, his eyes are black as night, Phoenix was in total control.

Phoenix: Let me go! She tried to kill our mate; I'll end her right now!!!

"Dad, wait! Look, she's moving, let mom do this I know she can!"

Tati stumbles leaning against a tree as she tries to shift, the shift is painful with the blade in. Kam pulls the blade, coughing up a bit of blood. She notices her wound isn't healing as fast as it should and looks at the blade coated in her blood, wiping it against the ground then inspecting it.

"Silver, that bitch laced the blade with silver."

P: Oh fuck this civil shit! All rules are now out the window since this bitch tried to cheat...

Kam's wound starts to glow purple and heal at the same time. Penelope had learned how to self-heal from poisons. Once restored, Penelope takes over, her eyes are different, they now have a fire-like essence. She stands tilting her head to the side, questioning Carolyn's sanity.

To buy time Carolyn launches the other three blades, she needs to hurt Kam in some way. Kam flicks her hand and all the blades shatter against the force field she put up in front of her.

"Tsk tsk tsk, Carolyn...I did exactly what you asked of me, to fight in my wolf and what did you do? You decided to cheat to win, you're weak just like your sister..."

"Shut up!"

"Such a sad...pathetic soul, worthy of nothing and no one, but cheer up Carolyn because soon you will be reunited with that bitch you call family. I thought I would feel a shred of sympathy for you but after what you just tried; I will still sleep soundly knowing that you're dead. Brady is my family now and he will go on to rule this pack with my daughter and her brother. I hope you realize your mistake, but you'll get no pity from me."

Carolyn's face doesn't waver, there's no sadness, no remorse, not even an ounce of guilt to all she had harmed including her own son and for that Penelope knew what she had to do.

She closes her fist, whispering a few words into it. She snaps her fingers and a mysterious black orb appears in the palm of her once closed hand, it has flashes of lightning within its swirling dark clouds. Kam smirked before she threw the orb, it absorbed into her body and she gasped. She touched where it entered and looked behind her. Nothing!

She scoffs, "Well, was that it?! What happened to the power of the Violet Legacy, you're getting weak in your old age."

It was Kam's turn to laugh, "Oh, Carolyn you see the thing about dark magic is you can make it bend to your will. You may have seen an orb just entering your body and feeling nothing but it's quite possibly the worst thing to ever happen. Goodbye, Carolyn, tell Bridget I said hello..."

Empervium santisi viopernium!

And with a snap of her fingers, the orb exploded, splattering Carolyn all over pack grounds. Not a distinguishable human body feature could be found.

Satisfied, Kam turns and walks towards her family whose mouths are wide open, Penelope had given her back control. She walks back as if nothing happened and she notices Kayd was pale and Kamden held Trini who couldn't look at the aftermath.

"Let's get groundskeeping and a cleaning crew to get this cleaned up ASAP and give them each a $5K bonus for this and tell them to tell no one. They have two hours, who knows when they'll come out, but I don't want them to see...that."

Kayd just shakes his head and is still so pale.

"Mom, that was totally badass!" Kamden yells as he puts his hand up for a high five and she returns it. Trini turns to her, her head still laying on his chest, "It was, Mrs. Miller but also just so...gruesome."

"Trini as you grow older and become a wife, mother, and what not you'll understand that patience can be fleeting. It was time to end this decades-old feud that I didn't even know I had, my family is safe, and my children are happy, that's all that matters."

She looks back at Kayd, who's color had started to return and so had his lust. "Baby doll, that was the hottest thing I've ever seen. I thought you fighting Bridget was hot, but this was so much better, albeit grisly. I'll spend every day for the rest of my life keeping you happy if it keeps you from doing that." He pulls her in, grabbing her waist.

Kamden starts pulling Trini toward the house. "Oh good grief, they're at it again, come on baby, let's go."

Kam smiles at Kayd, wrapping her arms around his neck pulling him in for a kiss. "Mmm, I don't think you could ever make me that mad unless you cheat or something, then I'll totally turn you into Jell-O."

He cringes, "Ugh, never eating that again. Come on, let's go inside while they clean up."

Going to the Chapel and...

(Six months later)

"This is crazy, Trini! What was I thinking?

Who allowed me to think this was a good idea?! I swear I'm going to pass out, this can't be good for the baby!"

Kay stood in front of the mirror; her bump prominent in her knee-length wedding dress. She adorned it with a short veil and white mary jane shoes.

She starts to hyperventilate, and Trini pulls her outside to the patio to get some fresh air. She navigates herself into the chair slowly. The view from their balcony gave them a bird's eye view of the entire Strip, from the water shows to the street performers and the touristy drunks here to experience Vegas.

"Oh, this is happening! I did not sit on a plane for hours to end up in Las Vegas to not see my best friend get married. You said you wanted this! Remember you'll have an intimate wedding at home later. Besides, my little Colden here kind of strengthens my case." Trini rubs her belly.

Kay was three months pregnant and because she was an Alpha and a Legacy her pregnancy period was much shorter; she was due in less than three months. If you had seen her walking by, you'd think she was near her third trimester.

Kay is still nervous and doubtful, her hands shaking. She looks at Trini, who was wearing a burgundy short flowy bridesmaid dress, her tears threatening to pour.

"I'm so nervous, Trin. What if he changes his mind or gets cold feet or he'll see how fat I've gotten?!"

"Honey, you are not fat, you are carrying his firstborn and if Brady had it his way you two would have been married long ago but your morning sickness kept you from that. As soon as the doctor cleared you, and found a local pack doctor here, he whisked you away to make you his wife! Sweetie, I'm sorry, but you're stuck with that amazing man for life."

She smiles, seemingly calming down and they share a laugh, "You're right, I can't believe it's finally happening! You're looking at the future Mrs. Preston! Now let's go, it's going to take me forever to get downstairs with this belly."

Trini grabs the bouquets and rings and they head out the door.

"Man, I can't believe our day is finally here, it couldn't come fast enough. My poor baby, the morning sickness took such a toll on her I was starting to get scared that something was wrong."

Brady continues to struggle with his tie.

"Hey, you don't need the tie. And my mom told me when she was pregnant with us that her morning sickness was so bad, she had to go on bed rest for a week, twice, so don't worry my sister is strong enough to handle this."

Den gave Brady a once over adjusting as he saw fit. Brady wore a burgundy smoker's jacket and black pants with a crisp black button-down, his hair slicked to the side as usual and black dress shoes.

Den stood beside him in the same but all black with burgundy lapels. His hair slicked back, a fresh style since Trini really liked it.

Brady started to breathe like he was in Lamaze class. "Dude, what are you doing? Calm down and breathe normally before you pass out, my sister would kill me!" He forces himself into slower, deeper breaths, his vision returning to normal. "I just can't believe I'm about to marry the girl of my dreams."

Outside the chapel doors, Kay stands with her bouquet of deep red roses. They did not choose one of those cheap gaudy drive-by chapels but chose a small chapel in the Venetian. The altar was intimate with white and gold accents all around, the only other color was burgundy, for him.

Trini squeezes her hand, "You ready? I'm going in!" She inhales deeply and nods. "More than ready for my happily ever after." Trini gives one last smile before the doors open for her to enter and close, so the groom doesn't see the bride and builds anticipation.

"You may now kiss your bride! Ladies and gentlemen, Mr. and Mrs. Brady Preston." Kamden and Trinity whoop and holler as he takes her in his arms, dipping her for their first kiss officially as husband and wife. He links her arm in his as Den and Trini throw confetti as they walk out.

When they open the chapel doors they stop in front of the elevator of the hotel while Trini and Brady switch keys.

Trini and Den were going to the casino to play for a bit before they hit a concert that happened to feature one of Trini's favorite artists.

Brady hugs his brother, "Have fun, maybe win a few million for the pack?"

"Yeah, I'll see what I can do but first I have to do something very important." They both nod in agreement.

Den turns to Trini and takes her hands. She looks confused as Brady pulls Kay into his side, whispering into her ear. She smiles and giggles as he reveals her brother's plan.

Den takes the opportunity of her disbelief by dropping to one knee, further shocking her.

"Trinity Sommer McCallister, one of the most beautiful girls I have ever laid eyes upon. You've been more than patient while I went through my want to be playboy phase, gallivanting, being girl crazy and you still waited for your time. You saw all my faults, yet you still loved me. I never spoke these words except to my family, but I love you more than you'll ever know. I didn't think I was worthy to have someone so special, but here you are, my beautiful angel."

By this time, she was in tears, sniffling as they drew a crowd.

"My amazing girl who lit up my life and gave me her heart, will you marry me?" He opens the ring box from his jacket pocket producing a brilliant three-carat diamond in a black onyx band. It was one of a kind, just like her.

Trini is speechless, her mouth was open but nothing distinguishable was coming out. Only squeaks and gasps.

"I-I....I uhh..."

Kay nudges her shoulder. "Trini, you've been waiting your whole life for him, say something!"

Den squeezes her hand as she notices the people looking on. There were smiles and grins and a few ladies were crying at the spectacle of love. She takes a deep breath, closing her eyes for a moment before locking onto his.

"Yes, Kamden Tristan Miller, I would love to be your wife! Yes! Yes! Yes!"

The crowd erupts as he places the ring on her finger, and he picks her up and spins her.

After the applause dies down a few people offer Kay and Brady their congratulations since it was obvious by their attire.

He kisses her temple, "I love you Mrs. Preston and I love you, Colden Miller Preston." He kisses her then bends to kiss her belly causing her to giggle.

"Is this what you hoped for, Brady?"

"No, I could never have wished for such a wonderful woman to carry my first-born son and love me beyond words. This is beyond my expectations and I'm excited to see what he inherits from your Legacy status. Do they have male witches?

"Yes dear, they're called warlocks."

He shrugs, "Sounds cool. We've been through a lot baby girl and we have so much more to go. I'm glad it all worked out in the end and even though no one will tell us what happened to my mom I am glad I don't have to deal with that anymore. I only have to worry about you and him." He rubs her stomach.

They reach their honeymoon suite and he carries her over the threshold.

"Are you ready to consummate our vows?"

"Well, I'm already knocked up."

"Doesn't mean we can't have fun practicing for the next Preston heir."

She rolls her eyes as he steps through the door.

THE END

Upcoming Release:

Unapologetically Nessa
(Character Backstory)

Chapter: Shots!

"WOOOOOOOOOOO!!!! SPRING BREAK! Bartender, get me six shots of tequila for me and my best friend here!"

Vanessa leans over the bar showcasing her perfectly plump boobs in her little black dress.

"Please..." She bites her lip to drive the point home and he quickly places the shots in front of her.

"No charge, beautiful." She grabs him by the neck and pulls him forward for a kiss.

"Thanks, lover boy." She writes her number down and slides it from his chest into his pants, but not his pocket, he gasps at her bold move.

"Don't lose it, you only get one chance." She winks as he walks away.

She looks over to her slightly intoxicated best friend.

"Nessa, I don't know if I can down three more, I can feel my liver dying!"

She passes over one of the six. "Don't worry, buddy, I'll take the remainder."

And she slams down two before a random cute guy asks her to dance. Kamari nods her approval indicating he was cute enough to dance with, if not more.

Nessa slides her shots to her. "Watch my babies until I get back." She giggles and makes her way to the dance floor of the only bar in town, Jack's.

It was a country saloon themed hangout which correlated to the small, quiet town that Lovingshire was. One horse town? There probably isn't a horse in a twenty-mile radius, all the ranches were north of here nestled near the mountains for easy access to the grazing trails.

Nessa enjoys the music more than the man, swinging her hips and dancing around always keeping an eye on her friend. She can't lie and say there wasn't an air of sadness when she saw her friend pine for true love. She was a beautifully old-fashioned girl and that is what made her a rare catch. Nessa on the other hand was more interested in having fun than finding love.

The stranger's hands went from her hips to around her butt and he squeezed making her squeal.

"Easy there, cowboy. I don't even know your name!"

He smiles pulling her hand up for a kiss. "Name's Dallas and yours, gorgeous?"

She scoffs loudly and goes back to her seat. Kam is shocked when she sees her leave him discarded on the dance floor, his face equally surprised.

"What the hell, Nessa? Why did you leave him there?"

She downs two shots, savoring the last one.

"Name was Dallas, you know how I feel about guys named after towns. Hard pass..." She takes the last shot and turns to observe the crowd.

Kam just shakes her head and completes her shot letting the burn pass without a chaser. "I know, but that specimen was drop dead gorgeous Nes, who cares if he was named after a town?"

Nessa rolls her eyes, "Remember Austin? Or Jackson, oh and Denver...he was a change of pace because I caught him with what was *his* name...hmm, oh, Jefferson! So no thank you to city named assholes." She downs her remaining shot and drags her best friend to the floor.

Kam and Nessa are soon the center of attention as they playfully grind on each other. Nessa takes notice of all the guys focused on them and decides to up the ante. She puts her hands-on Kam's hip playfully grinding against her. She swore she saw one guy drop his glass or at least she heard a glass drop.

Kam turns around and whispers, "Looks like you have a fan. Three o'clock with the red button down and wranglers."

She already rolled her eyes, wranglers screamed country boy which she wasn't really interested in, she wanted a motorcycle riding bad boy or even a sports car enthusiast, something that had nothing to do with her country surroundings. Country boys were a dime a dozen here, she needed change.

Curiosity overwhelmed her, and she turned to see the sexiest farm boy she's ever seen. He stood about six foot six with sapphire blue eyes and when their eyes met his lips pulled upward and accompanying his radiant smile were a set of dimples.

"Fuck me." She whispered, biting her lip.

"What?!"

She shakes her head "Not you, Mr. Dimples at the bar. He is absolutely gorgeous, oh yes, I'm going to enjoy this. Back me up, bestie."

Stay in Touch!

Email: **authormskeiya@yahoo.com**
FB Author Page: **www.facebook.com/authormskeiya**
Instagram:
www.intstagram.com/author_mskeiya
Bookbub:
www.bookbub.com/profile/s-courtney
Website (sign up for updates!): **scourtneybooks.com**

Please look out for the rest of the Bound Series and many more from S. Courtney

THE BOUND SERIES:
- Bound to You (#1)
- Bound by Destiny (#2)
- Blood Bound (#5)

CHARACTER BACKSTORIES:
- Unapologetically Nessa (#3)
- (Tentative Title) A Christian Tale (#4)

 # indicates release order

OTHER WORKS (Titles subject to change):
- The Black Aces MC
- Do You Want a 'Cup of Coffee?'
- Remember Me?
- It's Our Anniversary

www.ingramcontent.com/pod-product-compliance
Lightning Source LLC
Chambersburg PA
CBHW052021240626
47153CB00006B/1901